"Eric, what a
keep saying

"I saw Shawn today, Jamie."

The front tire of her bicycle wobbled dangerously. Jamie had to focus on the road ahead for a few minutes before she was able to talk again.

"I'm listening," she said.

"He showed up at my office, wanted to talk about... things. I thought it was the right opportunity to make Shawn really take notice. You remember how we talked about turning up the heat—"

"Eric, are you going to tell me what's going on or not?"

"Well...I just happened to mention to Shawn that... you and I are engaged."

"You what?!"

Dear Reader,

I'm somewhat of an expert on prewedding jitters. Cold feet preventing me from walking down the aisle, I balked on my wedding date not once, but twice—causing my future mother-in-law to throw up her hands in despair. But then I looked into my fiancé's eyes and reaffirmed what I'd known, deep down, all along: he truly was the perfect man for me, and we would have a wonderful life together navigating all the unknowns ahead. On a beautiful spring day I finally exchanged vows with him, and it's a decision I've never once regretted.

I've always wondered, though, what happens when regrets do get the better of "happily ever after." For example, when the groom changes his mind and ditches his bride, right at the altar...what's the bride to do? I had a great deal of fun exploring that question in *The Goodbye Groom.* After Jamie Williams is left holding the bridal bouquet, she decides to take matters into her own hands. Along comes Eric Sinclair, the groom's sexy brother....

I hope you enjoy reading Jamie and Eric's story as much as I enjoyed writing it.

Ellen James

THE GOODBYE GROOM

Ellen James

HARLEQUIN®

TORONTO • NEW YORK • LONDON
AMSTERDAM • PARIS • SYDNEY • HAMBURG
STOCKHOLM • ATHENS • TOKYO • MILAN • MADRID
PRAGUE • WARSAW • BUDAPEST • AUCKLAND

ISBN-13: 978-0-373-75140-2
ISBN-10: 0-373-75140-0

THE GOODBYE GROOM

This edition published by arrangement with Harlequin Books S.A.

www.eHarlequin.com

Printed in U.S.A.

ABOUT THE AUTHOR

Ellen James lives in New Mexico, "the land of enchantment," where she met the man of her dreams, and where she began her dream career—writing romance novels for Harlequin Books. Ellen shares a passion for history and the outdoors with her husband. The two of them are usually found poking around ghost towns, antique stores and classic auto shows, as well as hiking the gorgeous mountains of the southwestern United States.

Books by Ellen James

HARLEQUIN SUPERROMANCE

822—THE MAINE MAN
869—THE RESCUER
953—CHRISTMAS BABIES
1014—MY MONTANA HOME

Chapter One

He'll be here.

If she just kept repeating those words, they would be true. They had to be true.

Behind her, she heard scraps of whispers.

"...minister wants to know..."

"Should the organist play *that* again...?"

"Hasn't someone called him...?"

Then, at last, she heard the door to the bridal suite shutting and her mother coming to sit beside her. "I just knew he wouldn't show."

Jamie forced words past the tightness in her throat. "Mother, please. He'll be here."

"But...he's *not* here, Jamie. That's just the point. No groom...no word...no show..."

Jamie stood suddenly, the skirt of her wedding gown swirling around her. "He's late, that's all. You know how Shawn is. Can't keep time to save his life."

"Actually, I don't know. I mean, what do either one of us really know about him?"

Jamie clenched her hands, then realized she was

crushing her bouquet of pink roses and starflowers. Everything was perfect for her wedding day: the plaster-white walls of the old adobe church, the golden New Mexico sun streaming through the window, the dazzling blue of the sky. Only one ingredient was missing. The groom.

"If he's going to break your heart, best he do it now. Not wait until you've been married ten years—"

"Mother, stop, please." Jamie's throat ached now. "Don't make this about you and Dad."

Beyond the closed door, the sound of the organ came again, a forced march. How long could the woman play without the main event?

Jamie sank back down into her chair. She gazed at her mother, saw the lines of pride and bitterness etched into her face. Pride because Caroline Williams had managed to live almost twenty years without a man. Bitterness because she had never forgiven Jamie's father for walking out on her.

It won't happen to me. He'll be here.

"We have to do something, Jamie. This is becoming ridiculous."

She could no longer deny that much. Her fingers trembling just the slightest bit, Jamie punched the number of his cell phone. No response. Then his apartment number. The usual debonair "Shawn here" message on his answering machine had been replaced by another recording. "I'm sorry, Jamie." Just that, his voice subdued. *I'm sorry, Jamie.*

Very carefully she set down the phone. "Well," she said, surprised at the absolute calmness in her own voice. "At least we can tell that poor, wretched woman to stop playing her music." A deep breath. "There isn't going to be any wedding after all."

JAMIE COULD JUST imagine the headlines in the local newspaper: "Woman Arrested at Ex-Fiancé's Home." Of course, she didn't know if, strictly speaking, Shawn *was* her ex; his phone message had been so maddeningly obscure. And she wasn't exactly breaking into the house. She'd knocked at the door, then given in to the temptation to poke her head through a half-open window.

Why did she feel like such an intruder, then? Why did she know so little about the man she loved?

Jamie rested her arms wearily on the sill. Over the past twenty-four hours her usual levelheadedness had deserted her. Operating solely on emotion, she'd flown over a thousand miles to end up here at Saint-Anne—a tiny, unfamiliar island off the Washington mainland. *Never chase after a man,* her mother had warned her. Maybe Mom had been right.

Then again, Mom had been lonely most of her life.

"See anything you like?" asked a voice behind Jamie.

She started, straightening up so suddenly that she banged her head against the window frame. In all her twenty-eight years Jamie had never had so much as a dizzy spell. Not once during her tomboy days of bumps and bruises and broken bones. Not once during her years of flying. But now she was done in by a combination of hunger, exhaustion and the jolt to her head. The sky seemed to tilt, the ground to shift. Nothing steady remained. Even her stomach churned, a cold, sick sweat flushing her skin.

A hand caught her by the elbow. She found herself led along a pathway for a short distance and then lowered into a chair.

"Deep breaths," commanded the masculine voice. Strong fingers deftly probed the bump on her head. It was, admittedly, a rather pleasant sensation.

She would've laughed if she could. Yesterday she'd been a joyful bride-to-be. Today she was a certifiable wreck. But at last her ridiculous shakiness passed. The haze in front of her eyes cleared, and she saw a swimming pool off to her right with a flagstone patio curving around the back of the rambling shingled mansion. A glass of iced tea appeared before her. She sipped gratefully and focused on her rescuer. He was a man of considerable height, obliging her to crane her neck a bit.

Dark hair curling over a stern forehead. Aloof blue eyes. A Mediterranean heritage suggested by strong cheekbones and a deliberate jaw. A dash of France and Italy, a hint of Spain. Something exotic and dangerous. Something forbidding....

Jamie took another sip of the cold, spicy tea. She felt oddly disturbed by the man, unable to glance away from him. He gazed back at her assessingly, not saying a word.

"I'm looking for Shawn," she volunteered at last.

"Hmm...Shawn's not here," the man said.

A stab of disappointment went through her. "The ferry captain—he said Mr. Sinclair was in residence—"

"I suppose he meant me. I'm Eric Sinclair. Shawn's brother."

All Jamie could do was stare at him. "But he never said anything about a brother. I just assumed…" Her voice trailed off. One more thing she hadn't known about her fiancé. He'd seemed so open and giving yet ultimately had shared so little. And she'd done her best to ignore all her doubts about his reticence. She'd been in love…was *still* in love.

As she considered Eric Sinclair, she could see only a slight family resemblance. Perhaps the determined shape of the nose. And the confident stance—she recognized that. But *this* Sinclair had a gravity, a formal demeanor, even a certain grimness.

She sighed. "I'm Jamie Williams. Shawn and I—well, we were supposed to be on our honeymoon right about now."

The expression on Eric Sinclair's face was skeptical as he sat down across from her. His attire was more suited for a corporate boardroom than an island retreat. He wore a richly shaded charcoal suit and a silk tie slightly loosened. Almost unconsciously Jamie smoothed a wrinkle from her cotton skirt. Her rumpled condition, however, was the least of her worries.

"It seems your brother neglected a few items. Such as inviting you to the wedding…or bothering to show up at the altar."

Eric's look remained doubtful.

"He left a message for me," Jamie went on stubbornly. "He was sorry, he said. That's all—he was sorry. I don't even know what he meant. Is he sorry he ever met me? Sorry that he's hurt me? I need an explanation.

I *deserve* an explanation. When two people make promises to each other…that has to count for something. It might even be worth fighting for. Some things *are* worth the fight."

Eric loosened his tie a little more, as if preparing for a long story, yet there wasn't much left to tell.

"Your brother seems to have vanished from New Mexico, Mr. Sinclair. He'd told me about growing up on this island—I took a chance he'd be here." She paused. "Do you have any idea where he could be?"

"Ms. Williams, in the past I've cleaned up a fair share of my brother's messes. Swore I wouldn't do it again."

"I'm not somebody's *mess.*"

Eric passed a hand through his hair. "No, I don't know where he is."

"You probably wouldn't tell me even if you did know," Jamie stated flatly. "There's something you're not saying. Just come out with it, please."

"All right," he said in a beleaguered tone. "My brother has a habit of…attracting attention. Sometimes it's the family name, family wealth, whatever—"

He didn't need to spell it out. Jamie thumped her glass down on the poolside table. She stood, pushing her chair back so quickly it almost toppled over. "I understand," she said tightly. "You think I'm a—a gold digger. That's the term, isn't it? Let me tell you the truth. I don't give a damn about your family money, your family position, *whatever.* I just want your blasted brother to face me and tell me what's going on. And then I can tell *him* to go to…go to—" She couldn't finish. Blinded by foolish tears, she turned and began striding away. Her dignity wasn't helped when she stubbed her toe on a stone planter full of begonias.

Eric Sinclair came to the rescue again. He followed her, took hold of her arm and steered her back to one of the patio chairs. She grabbed a napkin from the table and impatiently swiped at her eyes. Eric stood in front of her, arms folded, looking more formidable than ever.

"I haven't accused you of anything, Ms. Williams," he said in a carefully expressionless voice. "Obviously you're upset. My brother has that effect on women, too."

She glared at him. "Shawn loves me. In spite of everything—I'm sure of that much. And that's why I'm really here."

Eric gave her a long, considering look. "You actually sound like you mean it. Maybe Shawn's done it this time."

"Done what?" she asked irritably.

He didn't answer her question, merely went on looking at her with a distracted frown. He gave the clear impression that he had other matters on his mind and she was an unwelcome nuisance. At last, though, he gave a shrug.

"There isn't another ferry until tomorrow at nine. I suppose you'll have to stay here for the night, get yourself sorted out."

She was used to being in control of her life, not someone who needed sorting out. "I've already registered at the hotel by the pier," she said stiffly.

He gave just a hint of a mirthless smile. "It's optimistic to call the Sand Castle a hotel. No...you'll stay here. Mrs. Braddock will take you to one of the guest rooms." He'd scarcely glanced toward the house when a sixtyish woman popped out a side door. She wore her graying hair in a ponytail, giving her a youthful appearance in spite of the fine lines etched into her face. Stepping closer, she treated Jamie to a frank perusal.

"You could do with a snack and then a rest before dinner," she pronounced.

It sounded like exactly what Jamie needed, but she didn't want to be managed—not by Eric Sinclair and not by this woman.

"I'll be fine at the hotel," she said. "My luggage is there already—"

"We'll see that it's delivered here," said Mrs. Braddock. "You don't want to stay at the Sand Castle."

Eric almost gave a genuine smile this time. "Resistance is useless. She's been running this family for years."

"Someone has to," the woman said crisply. She turned back to Jamie. "Come along, dear. I've made a blueberry pie."

The prospect of having a piece of that pie weakened Jamie's resolve—she hadn't eaten all day. But she stayed where she was, watching Eric Sinclair. He sat down at the table, unsnapped an expensive but clearly well-used briefcase and took out some files. He immersed himself in them, seeming to have dismissed her entirely.

The incongruity of the scene was too much. A man who could devote himself to business papers when the shimmering turquoise water of the pool beckoned from only a few yards away. Not to mention all the rest of it. The engagingly rustic house and the hills forested with pine, sweeping down to Puget Sound. Breathtaking. Yet there he sat, ignoring this gorgeous summer day as effectively as he ignored her. So unlike his brother Shawn, who took advantage of every opportunity to indulge…

"This way, miss," said Mrs. Braddock firmly. And Jamie, against her better judgment, ended up following.

SOME THINGS ARE WORTH *the fight.*

Those words wouldn't leave Eric in peace. Cursing under his breath, he tossed yet another report on the table. He'd been staring at these same numbers for fifteen minutes. Leaning back in his chair, he rubbed the kink in his neck. Shawn's latest escapade was already proving too much of a distraction.

Jamie Williams. Beautiful, passionate and angry. A potent combination.

Eric cursed again. It had been quite a while since he'd felt this distracted by a woman. Certain things tended to leave you numb: your wife announcing that she was going to leave you. Announcing that all along it had been your brother she'd wanted—and if she couldn't have him, see you later.

Eric stood, pacing in front of the pool. Surely he'd learned by now. Any woman connected to Shawn was strictly off-limits.

So why had he given in to that impulse and installed Jamie Williams in the house?

"I'm ready."

Eric turned at the sound of his daughter's voice. Seven-year-old Kaitlin hovered by the door, clutching a towel under her chin. She'd armed herself with all the necessary accoutrements: bathing suit, swim fins, snorkel. Every weapon possible to belie the fact that she was frightened of water.

Eric felt something twist inside him. It seemed impossible that you could love a daughter this much and still not know how to reach her.

An all-too-familiar guilt surfaced. He'd forgotten their appointment. That was how Kaitlin had phrased it—she'd requested an "appointment" with him, as if she were a business client instead of his child. And it had slipped his mind entirely.

"Hey there, sweet pea." Even as he spoke he knew his tone was too forced, too jocular. "Just have to change."

Kaitlin stared at him solemnly. There was no accusation in her gaze, just a somber recognition. Clearly she knew that he'd forgotten about their swimming lesson.

For the first few years of her life he'd been far too busy to be a good father. After the divorce, he'd vowed all that would change.

"I'll be right back," he said. "Mrs. Braddock will stay with you." Not that it was strictly necessary. Kaitlin's fear of the water would keep her safely away from the pool. Mrs. Braddock, however, appeared like a genie from the greenhouse, ponytail swishing. She was always available. Perhaps too available, Eric thought wryly. She'd done more to raise him and Shawn than their parents ever had.

He went inside and jogged up the stairs to the second story. Moving down the hall, he passed a half-open door. Something made him slow down and turn back. He stood at the door, gazing inside one of the guest rooms.

Jamie Williams lay on the bed, fast asleep. In this

light he could see the freckles scattered lightly across her cheeks and the bridge of her nose. Her red hair fanned against the pillow. He felt like a damn voyeur, but he just stood there…thinking all the wrong things about a woman who looked good in all the right ways.

What the hell was he doing? She'd come here searching for his brother. At last, Eric turned and strode to his own room. Only a few more moments and he'd changed into his swimming trunks.

Back down at the pool, he sat at the shallow end and beckoned to his daughter.

Kaitlin remained where she was, standing stiff and silent beside the housekeeper.

"Hmm…I have something to do in the kitchen," Mrs. Braddock murmured diplomatically before she disappeared. Now Kaitlin stood all alone, clutching her towel.

"It's okay," Eric said. "Today we'll just dangle our feet again."

She inched closer to the pool, her eyes large and dark in her small face. Since the divorce, Eric's seven-year-old daughter had taken it as a point of honor to confront her fears—fear of the water, of darkness, of school….

Her fear of water had been the most challenging. So far nothing had worked. Private instruction, lessons at the community-center pool…even Mrs. Braddock's comforting ways had had no effect. Every effort had ended in misery and tears. For Kaitlin, the water seemed to contain unnamable demons. Yet, the greater her trepidation, the more she seemed determined to struggle against it. These sessions with Eric were always at her own request.

He moved his feet in the water. "Nice and cool," he remarked.

Kaitlin tiptoed closer. She spread out her towel next to him and sat down. For a long moment she stared at her pink flip-flops. Then she slipped them off and stuck a few tentative toes into the water.

"Good," Eric told her.

"It's the same thing we did last time."

"So?"

"So we haven't made any *progress*," she said scornfully.

"Sure we have. Two weeks ago you wouldn't even stand this close."

His comment earned him a resigned look. She stuck both feet into the water, sitting there rigidly. If her comfort factor seemed low, at least she'd made it this far. How could he convince her it was an accomplishment?

"You know," he said conversationally, "I'm going to Seattle in a few days. You could come with me again. After work, we'll go up the Space Needle. You can even stop by and visit your mom."

"I'd rather not," she answered all too quickly, ducking her head.

"Kaitlin," he said as gently as possible. "You can't avoid your mom much longer. She misses you."

Kaitlin raised her head and stared at him with those enormous brown eyes. He saw the glisten of tears.

"Then why," she mumbled, "did Mom divorce us?"

His daughter could get to him in a second. He put his arm around her, wishing he could protect her from every hurt.

"She didn't divorce you, honey—just me. She loves you."

Kaitlin blinked hard. She pulled away, her feet coming out of the pool with a splash. Her toes burrowed toward the pink flip-flops as if seeking refuge.

"We're not making any progress at *all,*" she said, her voice trembling dangerously.

"You're doing fine—"

"You *know* I'm not. What's the point of lying?" She stared at him accusingly. Where had she learned to be so hard on herself? And why didn't he know how to comfort her?

She marched across the patio and disappeared inside the house. Eric knew that she'd find some measure of solace with Mrs. Braddock in the kitchen. But that wasn't good enough, not by far. A daughter should be able to count on her dad.

Eric debated following her, but lately the pattern had always been the same: he tried to be a good father; she pushed him away.

So he wasn't trying hard enough, dammit. He had to come up with something better, and soon. Pacing to the table, he stared broodingly at the files scattered there. He was supposed to be working on the Garrett buyout. If he couldn't be the right father, at least he should be focusing on business.

Instead he sat down and took another folder from his briefcase. He opened it and gazed at the rough sketches he'd made not so long ago. With a finger he traced the lines of his dream. His fantasy.

It would remain a fantasy, of course. He was too

much a realist to believe anything else. But for now he could escape the problems confronting him: a family business that had begun weighing all too heavily upon his shoulders; a daughter who ran from him; a brother who'd ditched a fiancée.

Right now Eric could forget all that as he gazed at the pages before him.

He could dream.

Chapter Two

Jamie stirred, opening her eyes slowly. At first she couldn't remember where she was. Albuquerque...anticipating her wedding day...

Reality brought her fully awake. There'd been no wedding. She was on the small island of Saint-Anne, Washington, trying to find the reluctant groom.

Jamie swung her legs over the side of the bed. With a heartfelt sigh she padded to the window and gazed outside. The first shadows of evening had begun to drift over the patio below. Eric Sinclair sat at the poolside table, legs stretched out comfortably. Instead of his too-severe business attire, he wore a bathing suit. Jamie could see the breadth of his shoulders, the dark hair curling across his chest, the well-proportioned muscles along every inch of his body.

She drew back—but only a little. Something obliged her to remain where she was, hidden by the curtains, staring downward with a half-guilty fascination. The man, after all, was her fiancé's brother.

Ex-fiancé, she told herself acidly. Nonetheless, it

seemed wrong to study Eric Sinclair when he was so unaware of her scrutiny. His attention centered completely on the sheaf of papers he held. A smile played across his mouth, all sternness vanished.

A scuffling noise made Jamie turn her head. She saw a young girl peering at her from the hallway, a child with dark tumbled hair and curious brown eyes.

"Come in," Jamie said encouragingly.

The child slid inside the room—but only just. She wore shorts and an oversize shirt emblazoned *Seattle Mariners*. As she folded her arms, her stance suggested fragility and defiance all at once.

"Are you my dad's girlfriend?"

For one crazy, absurd moment Jamie wondered if there was something else she didn't know about her exfiancé. Good Lord, did Shawn have a *daughter* he'd neglected to mention?

The dark-haired little girl seemed to lose her resolve and began inching back toward the hallway.

"Hmm...I don't know who your dad is," Jamie remarked, "but I imagine he's someone very important. Someone like...the president of the United States."

The child paused. She gave Jamie a speculative glance.

"Okay," Jamie said. "Let me guess. He's more like...the king of Spain."

The child remained perfectly solemn, her large brown eyes intent as she studied Jamie.

"Maybe," Jamie said, "he's more like...the emperor of Japan."

The little girl pressed a finger to her mouth as if to keep a smile from escaping. She slid toward the window and gazed downward. Jamie followed the direction of her gaze to Eric Sinclair, who was still oblivious to the summer's beauty surrounding him. Still absorbed in the papers he held.

"So that's your dad," Jamie said very seriously. "I was right—he is someone important."

The child watched her father for another moment, her expression grave. She seemed absorbed by her thoughts, and Jamie did not try to interrupt. Then, elusive as quicksilver, the little girl slipped away from the window and out of the room.

At the very last moment the child peered back at Jamie. The unspoken message was understood: Jamie could follow if she chose.

The little girl led the way down the hall to another room. Here was a lively clutter: toys scattered across the floor, stuffed animals sprawled on the bed, books piled haphazardly on shelves. The child knelt beside a wicker basket. She reached inside and gently scooped up a kitten—all black except for its white left front paw.

"This is Isabel. You can hold her if you want."

"Thank you," said Jamie. She sat down on the floor beside the little girl and cradled the scrap of fur, listening to it purr. "Isabel...quite a lofty name for someone so cute. Where'd you get her?"

"My dad."

Jamie tried to picture Eric Sinclair choosing this adorable little kitty as a gift for his daughter.

"I'm Jamie, by the way."

The little girl glanced away as if suddenly unsure again. "I'm Kaitlin," she offered after a second. Then she jumped up and went to her desk, where a set of watercolors was prominently displayed. She brought a few pictures to place silently in front of Jamie.

"Here," said Jamie. "I'll trade." She handed over the tiny Isabel so that she could take a closer look at the pictures. "Hmm…a good likeness." The kitten was depicted rather larger than life, with so much black paint that the paper had crinkled. "And who's this?"

"My dad."

His daughter had placed him on the very edge of the page, in a business suit with lopsided tie.

"I'll bet," Jamie said, "your father's the one who gave you these paints."

Kaitlin didn't answer, simply ducked her head over the kitten. Jamie studied another picture.

"Can you tell me about this one?"

"That's our pool," Kaitlin said, her voice so soft that Jamie had to strain to hear. Then the child lifted her head, and the expression in her big, dark eyes was surprisingly mournful. "That's me," she said almost in a whisper. "That's me…hating the water."

After this bleak statement, Jamie gave the picture a more thorough perusal. It depicted a small solitary figure huddled to the side as if to escape the threatening expanse of dark blue.

Kaitlin seemed to have run out of words. She sat down on the carpet but at some distance from Jamie. Her head bent over the kitten once more.

Jamie chose her next words with care. "Water can be scary," she acknowledged. "You never know what it's going to do. It might start…splashing."

The little girl raised her head cautiously and regarded Jamie.

"The water," Jamie said, "might start...crashing."

Kaitlin lifted her eyebrows just a fraction.

"Or maybe," Jamie went on, "the water might start...dashing."

Kaitlin pressed a hand to her mouth as if to prevent the escape of another wayward smile, but then it appeared she could not resist. She lowered her hand. "The water," she said, "might start...prancing. Or maybe it might start...dancing." Her eyes seemed to dance, expressing genuine delight. But then all too quickly she grew solemn again, as if worried that somehow she'd let down her guard too much. There was something about this child's gravity, the serious expression on her delicate little face that reminded Jamie of herself long ago, when she'd been a little older than Kaitlin, struggling with the fact that the world could simply not be trusted anymore. How could it, when her father had simply gone out the door one morning and not come back?

Jamie swallowed past a sudden tightness in her throat. She knew too well how vulnerable a child could be. And that was what she saw in Kaitlin's large brown eyes.

Vulnerability.

THAT EVENING, ERIC SAT at the dining room table and watched as Mrs. Braddock performed the finishing touches on her dinner presentation. She straightened the silverware, folded one of the snowy napkins more precisely, rearranged the centerpiece of daisies and carnations. Then she stood back and observed the gleaming china plates with satisfaction.

"We'll have to entertain more often," Eric remarked. "You seem to be enjoying yourself."

She gave him a sharp glance. "No harm in a little festivity." She turned with a huff and arranged the draperies so the late sun would fall at just the right angle. Then she muttered something under her breath.

Eric rubbed his neck. He knew from long experience that Mrs. Braddock had something on her mind. When she started rumbling like this, she was like a volcano itching to erupt—if only she had a little encouragement.

"Didn't quite catch that, Mrs. B."

"Pigweed and prickly lettuce," she declared. "Ring a bell?"

He didn't have a clue what she was talking about and he'd started to regret that he'd asked. But, also from long experience, he knew there was no way out of it.

"Hey, just as long as it's not something we're having for dinner," he said.

She gave him a severe look, clearly not appreciating his attempt at humor. "Your brother, fifth-grade science project, homemade mulch and weed control."

Mrs. B. had an impressive memory. It seemed she could recall every one of their school projects—as well as every one of their childhood infractions.

"It's coming back to me," he said. "Shawn really got involved with that one. Piles of mulch everywhere."

Mrs. B. nodded. "Your brother gave it everything he had—until the very night of the fair. He was scared. Scared he wouldn't win first place. Anything less... So he dumped the whole thing into the drink and didn't even go."

"Just like he didn't show up at the altar," Eric remarked. "Fear of failure—it's a hypothesis, Mrs. B. As long as we're talking scientific method, though, other possibilities have to be considered."

"Ha." She gave him another repressive glance, then, with a bounce of her ponytail, she was gone.

Shawn's fear of failure... But Shawn wasn't exactly a kid anymore, and sooner or later he had to solve his own problems. This time he'd outdone himself, leaving a beautiful, inconvenient redhead in his wake.

Speaking of Jamie Williams, she had yet to appear. Not to mention that Eric's daughter was also conspicuously missing. He sat alone at the dining room table with all this splendor before him.

Eric glanced at his watch, then felt angry at himself. Too much of his life had been run by a damn clock. Hadn't he promised to change for Kaitlin's sake? What she needed was time...*his* time. That was why he'd brought her here this summer, to the house where he'd grown up.

Okay, maybe that had been something of a mistake. This place was too full of memories, the discomforting kind. How many strained dinners had he suffered through in this very room? The empty chair at the head of the table, waiting for his father. His mother, withdrawn into her own private thoughts. Shawn, a funny, anxious little kid back then, trying to pick a fight with Eric just so there'd be some noise in the place. And maybe, finally, Dad arriving, and the unspoken question weighting the air: what would be his mood this time...?

Impatiently Eric pushed back his chair and stood. Something else occurred to him now. From long habit, he'd dressed formally for dinner—jacket, tie and all. It had been the custom in this house when he was a boy. Whenever he was here, he fell too easily into the old ways. The past was over. His daughter needed him to focus on the future.

But where was she, anyway?

Muffled sounds from outside drew him. The murmur of voices, an odd clink, a subdued splash. He went to the back door and stood gazing toward the pool. An inexplicable sight greeted him: Jamie Williams and his daughter carefully lifting up one of the patio tables between them and pitching it into the shallow end of the pool. Two patio chairs had already been deposited in the water. Jamie slipped off her sandals, waded in and captured one of the chairs. She positioned it just so in front of the table.

After a moment's hesitation, Kaitlin waded into the shallow end, too. She looked completely absorbed, grabbing hold of the other chair cushion to keep it from floating off into the deeper part of the pool.

Eric leaned in the doorway, continuing to watch. It would be reasonable to ask why his daughter and his brother's fiancée were giving the patio furniture a dunking. Maybe the answer didn't matter all that much, though. Not when his daughter was actually in the pool, braving the water. A minor miracle.

Eric's gaze strayed to Jamie Williams. She was standing in his pool fully clothed, but even this ridiculous circumstance did not make her any less alluring.

Perhaps more so. She rested her arms on the back of the chair and bent down to catch something Kaitlin was saying. The breeze played with her red hair, while the late-evening sun gave a golden cast to her skin. Her skirt draped damply. With a little imagination, she might have been a lovely Greek statue brought to life. Aphrodite rising from the sea....

What was wrong with him? He made a restless gesture and propelled himself away from the doorway. Jamie and Kaitlin turned at the same moment and caught sight of him.

A variety of emotions seemed to flicker across Jamie's expressive face. Guilt, confusion, perhaps humor at her own predicament. But it was his daughter's expression that really got to him. She stared at him defiantly, as if expecting the worst. Expecting that he wouldn't understand, wouldn't tolerate the unpredictable, that his first reaction would be to chastise.

Had the divorce led to this—Kaitlin distrusting him so automatically now? And what the hell was he going to do about it?

Jamie broke the awkwardness. She sat down in her chair in front of the table—sat there in the pool, water eddying around her, as if it were the most normal thing in the world. Kaitlin studied her before she, too, sat down, elbows at the table. Both of them now stared calmly at Eric. Clearly the next move was up to him.

Jamie Williams had been here scarcely a few hours and already she had disturbed the waters in more ways than one. Eric felt as if he were facing some obscure test, one he might easily fail in his daughter's eyes.

There was nothing to do but jump in—literally and figuratively. Eric sat down at the pool's edge and made an elaborate procedure of untying his shoes, taking off his socks. Kaitlin's eyes seemed to grow larger as she watched, but she didn't say a word. He loosened his tie, took off his jacket and tossed it onto the tiles. Then he picked up his own patio chair, waded into the pool with it and sat down next to his daughter. Her brown eyes widened a bit more.

Mrs. Braddock appeared. She folded her arms and observed the lot of them, admirably impassive.

"Mrs. B.," said Eric. "Tonight, if you don't mind, we'll have dinner…in the pool."

Something seemed to glimmer in Kaitlin's eyes. But then, as so often happened these days, her head dipped forward and a protective curtain of hair fell across her face.

Eric still didn't know if he'd passed the test, but he was determined to keep on trying. So he behaved as if dinner à la pool was something he did every day. He waded up and down the pool steps to deliver Mrs. B.'s delicious offerings: roasted peppers and eggplant, homemade rolls, shepherd's cheese, pasta with basil sauce. Mrs. Braddock had even brought two candles for an air of festivity; he lit them and placed them in the center of the table. Mrs. B. herself retreated as if grateful to escape.

Eric sat down, serving Kaitlin extra sauce on her pasta.

"Thank you, Dad," she said formally. He tried to remember the last time she'd called him by the more casual term of "Pops." He missed that. Before his marriage to Leah had ended, even when he hadn't been the most involved of fathers, he'd still been able to count on a hug from Kaitlin, as well as her smile or laughter. And, yes, a beleaguered but affectionate "Oh, Pops" on occasion. But ever since the divorce…

Would his daughter's life always be divided in this painful way?

Jamie Williams seemed to be focusing rather intently on her plate, no doubt sensing unspoken tensions. Eric poured his daughter some cranberry-grape juice.

"Thank you, Dad."

Maybe if he'd been closer to her from the very beginning, the split wouldn't have been so traumatic for her. Maybe she'd have a more solid foundation on which to build. It occurred to Eric that his life was full of *maybes* these days. Although Kaitlin had never been a particularly bold child, she'd once seemed at ease in her surroundings. It was only after the divorce that the insecurities had started to surface. The fear of darkness, for one, and the fear of water…and of school.

Yet she didn't seem fearful at the moment. She moved her feet back and forth, sending up a shower of droplets.

"Jamie," she said comfortably, "would you pass the applesauce, please?"

Jamie obliged. "I think I'll have a little more myself."

"I like apples," said Kaitlin.

"So do I," Jamie replied. "Apples are my favorite fruit."

"What's your favorite cookie?"

"Hmm…it's a tie between chocolate-chip and coconut-macaroon."

"Chocolate-chip is definitely the best," Kaitlin pronounced.

"You just might be right."

Eric listened to this interchange. Kaitlin was behaving as if she'd known Jamie Williams forever.

"Oatmeal-raisin is my favorite," he murmured to no one in particular, and *no one* responded.

"Maybe I'll have a little more of that applesauce, too," he added.

"Here you go, Dad." Kaitlin passed the bowl and then turned back to Jamie. "What's your favorite vegetable?"

"Caramel corn," Jamie said without missing a beat.

Kaitlin's eyes sparkled. "*That's* not a vegetable!"

"Oops," said Jamie and smiled at her.

Kaitlin almost smiled in return.

Eric knew when he'd been upstaged. He settled back in his chair and watched Kaitlin with his brother's fiancée…ex-fiancée? These past few months Kaitlin had clearly been struggling with a weight of fear and uncertainty. But now, at this moment, he sensed almost a lightness to her attitude.

He had to admit there was something unique about Jamie Williams. The way she treated his daughter with such seriousness—and yet at the same time with such a flair for nonsense. By now, Kaitlin and Jamie had moved on to a discussion of favorite animals.

"Kittens," said his daughter, "are *my* favorite."

"Well, of course. Isabel would be highly offended if she thought otherwise."

"What's your favorite?"

"Monkeys," said Jamie. "Definitely. Because they appreciate the many fine attributes of bananas and because they know how to make faces."

Kaitlin immediately scrunched up her nose. "Like this?"

"No, more like this." Jamie reached over and gently tickled Kaitlin into a small giggle. His daughter almost sounded carefree.

Jamie Williams had been here only a few hours. In that brief time, she'd managed to charm Kaitlin with a sense of magic, a delight in the absurd. Eric had to admit those qualities had been in short supply around the Sinclair household lately.

In fact, Jamie had reminded him of just how much was missing here. Laughter, lightheartedness. And, yes, magic.

Chapter Three

Dinner finished, Jamie set her fork down regretfully. She couldn't remember the last time she'd had quite so satisfying a meal. When the housekeeper appeared poolside a few moments later, Jamie told her as much.

"You're a wonderful cook, Mrs. Braddock."

"Yes, absolutely wonderful," said Kaitlin, sounding very grown-up. The corner of Mrs. B.'s mouth gave a twitch, but otherwise she acknowledged the compliments with a brisk, professional nod.

"All right," she said. "Front and center—everyone under the age of twenty can help me with the dishes."

Kaitlin stole a peek at Jamie.

"No way—I plead the fifth," Jamie told the little girl, as deadpan as possible. "As we know, a woman never discusses her age."

Kaitlin seemed to consider this and then nodded in solemn agreement. She began gathering the cups and silverware while Eric stacked the plates. The two Sinclairs worked efficiently together. Whenever Eric glanced at his daughter, the tenderness in his eyes was clear. Yet perhaps there was a glimpse of puzzlement, as well. He seemed to be asking questions of himself, immersed in private musings, and Jamie suddenly felt like an intruder in this little family circle. To cover her sense of loneliness and confusion, she busied herself by helping to transport the dishes topside to Mrs. Braddock's tray.

Now Kaitlin padded across the patio, trailing Mrs. B. As the two of them reached the door to the house, Mrs. B.'s voice came faintly. "All right. Everyone who has wet feet can dry them on this towel."

Jamie and Eric remained seated at the table, their own legs still submerged. The water was pleasant, even as the shadows of evening lengthened around them. The master of the house had said nothing about her rearranging the furniture, and she gave him credit for that. He behaved as if it were perfectly normal to sip after-dinner wine quite literally alfresco. And yet his presence disconcerted her, had done so since the first moment she'd met him. Maybe it was that she hadn't even known of his existence until today. Why *hadn't* Shawn mentioned Eric? What strains between two brothers could lead to such an omission?

In the short time Jamie had been in the Sinclair home she'd discovered a few facts on her own. It was clear that Eric Sinclair loved his daughter very much. It was equally clear that Kaitlin loved her dad very much. Yet the two of them seemed to have just a bit of trouble connecting. They both seemed to share an elemental reserve.

At times Kaitlin seemed on the verge of relaxing. But then she'd hold back, as if afraid to indulge—as if afraid that happiness and security could all too easily be snatched away.

Jamie believed she understood at least some of Kaitlin's uncertainty. This afternoon, Mrs. Braddock had let slip a few details about Eric Sinclair. A recent difficult divorce, tense custody arrangements. It was a story familiar to Jamie from her own childhood. Even under the best of circumstances it hurt deeply. And the circumstances, perhaps, could never be the best.

Even when a father cared for his daughter as much as Eric Sinclair evidently did.

Jamie took a sip from her wineglass. Eric hadn't spoken for several minutes. The light of the candles flickered between them on the table. Eric's face remained in shadow, obscured by the growing night, yet he still managed to dominate his surroundings. There was nothing easy about him, nothing restful. As soon as his daughter had gone with Mrs. B., he'd reverted to the forbidding demeanor of this afternoon.

Then it occurred to her how things had been exactly the opposite with Shawn. It had been so easy to be swept up in dreams of love and a new life. Until the moment, of course, when he had neglected to show up at the altar.

"It's getting late," she said. "And it has been a long day."

"You can't turn in," Eric said, "until you come clean. How did you get my daughter into the water? Beyond throwing my furniture into the brink, what's the rationale?"

Jamie turned her wineglass in one hand, staring at the reflection of the candlelight. "Simple. I just told her the truth. I told her that when I was a little older than her I was deathly afraid of flying. But I was going to visit my father for the first time since my parents' divorce, and the only way to do that was to get on that plane...." She was telling too much. She had to stick to the point. "So, I decided I would combine something I loved with the thing that I hated. I grabbed my favorite Nancy Drew mystery and stuck my head in it for the entire flight. Sure enough, by the end, I hardly even knew I was flying. And then, after the next flight and the next, I wasn't so afraid anymore."

Jamie set down her glass, watching as Eric filled it again. She was already perhaps too intoxicated by the northwestern air, the mysteriousness of this night. "Anyway," she continued, "I suggested to Kaitlin that she try the same technique—associate something she wasn't afraid of with the pool. She told me that she was hungry and that she certainly wasn't afraid of dinner."

Eric filled his own glass and took a thoughtful sip. "You have a novel approach, Ms. Williams—Jamie. And I happen to be grateful."

For some reason, she didn't want his gratitude. She hadn't helped Kaitlin for that, anyway. She'd simply responded to the moment, with a little girl who reminded her of herself as a child.

"Simple psychology," she said. "It worked for me, in any case. I grew to love flying instead of hating it. Even started taking lessons so I could get my pilot's license." She didn't want to talk about herself to this man, so why was she doing it? Yet he'd learn certain facts soon enough. She couldn't hide them. "Flying was how I met your brother," she went on. "Eventually I became a flight instructor myself. He signed up for lessons. End of story."

"Interesting way to put it." Eric's voice betrayed no emotion. He and his daughter were very much alike indeed, both reluctant to expose their feelings.

Unfortunately the turbulent events of the past few days had shattered any reserve on Jamie's part. She found herself speaking again.

"The point is, I could tell right away your brother was a genuinely warm person. We started dating, and by the time we were engaged I knew he wanted a home and a family as much as I did—" She stopped herself but not in time. She was definitely revealing too much.

Eric shifted in his chair, as if he, too, regretted her revelations. "Look, Jamie. I sense you're telling me this because you want me to convince you of something. Maybe you want me to tell you that you didn't make a mistake where Shawn's concerned. Hell, I'm not going to argue with you about my brother's better qualities. He does have them. But he's the one you need to speak to."

"That's why I came here. I just need to talk to him. And after that…" She didn't know what would happen afterward. She didn't seem to know anything about her life anymore.

Jamie set down her glass and stood. "It really has been a long day. I'll say good night, Mr. Sin—Eric."

He rose to stand beside her. "For what it's worth," he said, "I'm sorry about my brother."

"Thank you," she said tightly.

She and Eric both moved at the same time, the water eddying around them. She intended to climb the pool steps and go to the house; he no doubt meant to let her pass. But it didn't end up that way. Somehow they were facing each other and Eric's hand was on her arm.

It should have been a meaningless, accidental touch, a mistake in the darkness. Yet it sent a disconcerting warmth all through her, made her draw in her breath. Dismayed, she found herself gazing up at him. But he was still enclosed by the shadows, not even the light spilling from the windows of the house able to reach him.

Then, just as suddenly as it had happened, it was over. He stepped back, murmured a good-night, and she was on her way toward the house, her bare, damp feet moving across the stones of the patio, her sandals dangling from her hand. Her breath still rose and fell unsteadily.

Surely it had only been the effect of wine and weariness and heartache. She'd been left at the altar—no wonder all her reactions seemed heightened. But she didn't need to spend any more time with the groom's brother.

What she needed was to find the groom.

THE NEXT MORNING Jamie zipped up her duffel and swung her carry-on bag over her shoulder. This was the sum total of her luggage. She'd always been the type to travel light—and yesterday even more so. Racing to catch a runaway fiancé, a person had a tendency to ignore the finer details of packing.

She couldn't stop now. She'd come this far to demand her explanation from Shawn and she had to keep looking for him. She needed to learn the truth or she'd have no hope of getting on with her life.

Why did you walk out on me? Why did you leave, just like my dad all those years ago...?

He wasn't here to answer her questions. That was why she had to take the next step—go to Seattle. Mrs. Braddock, in her sensible, straightforward manner, had suggested last night that Shawn would be found there. Consequently, Jamie had fortified herself with her favorite dress, a tailored style in turquoise silk.

Now she went quickly down the stairs and out of the house to the driveway, where a dark blue truck waited. Mrs. Braddock helped her put her bags in the back. The housekeeper was about to climb into the driver's seat when Eric appeared.

"Thank you, Mrs. B.," he said. "I'll take over from here."

Mrs. Braddock gave him a considering glance, apparently not intimidated in the least by his stern demeanor. She tossed him the keys, gave a brisk farewell to Jamie and disappeared inside. Jamie glanced upward, wondering if, for just a second, she'd seen Kaitlin's heart-shaped face hovering at one of the windows. Jamie waved, but now the window was blank. Why did she feel this sudden ache inside? It made no sense at all—she scarcely knew the child.

A few moments later Eric was driving Jamie down the hill, the dazzling waters of the Sound sparkling before them. At first she made no effort at conversation. She told herself simply to gaze straight ahead. Another few moments and she would probably never see Eric Sinclair again. There was no reason to feel this unsettling awareness. Last night she'd been able to blame it on wine and exhaustion. This morning she could only blame it on the fact that she *had* been ditched at the altar.

Did she want to get back at Shawn for what he'd done to her? Being attracted to Shawn's brother, there would be a revenge....

She shook her head. If only it were that simple. She sensed something far more in her confused emotions, something unexplainable. The sooner she got away from Eric Sinclair, the better.

Reluctantly, she found herself studying his profile. The man was unquestionably attractive. The strong, definitive lines of his face suggested the force of personality she was already coming to know. His thick dark hair curled just a bit over his collar, conveying a certain rebellion. He was not someone who would fit neatly into any category. Yesterday's sophisticated business suit had implied that he was an executive. Today, however, he wore shorts and a polo shirt and he was driving a vehicle well suited to the lush, wild greenery of the island.

Jamie realized that she was staring and forced her gaze forward. "I'd expect a sports car from you," she said. "Something that could get you anywhere fast."

"What makes you think I like to drive fast?" He sounded faintly amused.

"Just a hunch. I have a feeling you don't like anything—or anyone—to get in the way."

"Maybe I should just drive a bulldozer."

Jamie almost smiled at that. She couldn't help herself—she looked at him again and saw a hint of humor playing about his mouth.

"I have plans for this truck," he said. "I'm thinking about getting a camper. Kaitlin's mentioned that she'd like to go camping."

"Let me guess. She mentioned that she liked cats, and you got her a kitten."

"Lord, am I that pathetic?" he asked. "I throw presents at my daughter and hope it'll make her love me."

Neither of them spoke for a few seconds. Then Eric gave a slight, impatient shrug.

"The divorce was hard on her."

"It's hard for any child."

"That's right, you speak from experience."

She'd definitely revealed too much last night, but now more slipped out. "I was nine years old when my parents broke up. It was very messy, nothing civil about it. My mother has yet to move on. So, yes, I understand what it's like."

Lost in her thoughts, it took Jamie a minute to realize that they'd turned right instead of left toward the pier.

"I'll be late," she said.

"Don't worry—I'll get you to the ferry in plenty of time." Eric drove down one street and then another, ending up in front of a building of mellowed brick that had the words *Ulysses Elementary* lettered in stone above the wide front doors. Since it was summer, no children were about. Eric cut the engine.

"What are we doing here?" Jamie asked.

"Not sure myself. Just followed an impulse."

"I doubt," she said, "that you follow impulses very often."

He leaned back in his seat, one hand resting on the steering wheel. "I seem that dull to you?"

Definitely not dull. Enigmatic, disturbing, irritating...but not dull in the least.

"I only meant that you're a focused sort of person. I'm sure you have other things to do today."

He gazed broodingly toward the school. "There's always something else to do," he murmured almost to himself. "That's the way it is now. That's the way it was when Shawn and I were kids. One or the other of us always messing up somehow. Not measuring up."

Jamie didn't speak. Eric seemed lost in his own memories, and she did not want to intrude. Then he stirred and addressed her once more.

"This is the school Shawn and I both went to. Did he tell you about Mrs. Green's reign of terror in the third grade?"

Jamie sighed. "He didn't tell me about you, so he certainly didn't tell me about his school days." It was humiliating, really. When you were going to marry someone, you were supposed to know all those little stories about him—his third-grade teacher, the friends he'd had, the friends he'd lost. Why hadn't she noticed that Shawn had been less than forthcoming about his past and family? Had she been so blinded by her own emotions? Why hadn't she persisted whenever Shawn had so adroitly changed the subject? And why, most of all, hadn't he wanted to share with her?

"I'm lucky I even know he grew up here," Jamie said. "It's as if he never wanted me to know the ordinary facts and details of his life. As if somehow that would give me too much control over him."

"I'll fill in the blanks, then. Mrs. Green scared us all to death. Yet, when I broke my arm falling off the wall out back, she's the one who drove me to the hospital.

Nobody could reach my parents, so she just took charge. Kept telling me stories about her own son so I'd forget how much it hurt. That's when I first discovered that people aren't always what they seem."

A breeze drifted through the open windows of the truck. Jamie settled back in her seat, gazing toward Eric's school but seeing her own childhood.

"Third grade," she said. "Third grade is when I beat up Charlie Henderson. I found him pouring water down an anthill and I soon put a stop to that. Got sent to the principal's office afterward."

"Defender of the weak and innocent," Eric observed with a smile.

"Not according to my mom. She said you didn't pummel boys no matter what the reason. Maybe you weren't supposed to trust them, but you weren't supposed to beat up on them, either. You were just supposed to make darn sure one of them never broke your heart."

"Did you listen?"

"Apparently not or I wouldn't be here."

"Did my brother break your heart, Jamie?" Eric asked quietly.

She clenched her hands in her lap. "Yes—I don't know. Right now I just think I hate him."

"Hating someone usually means you still care…a lot."

How could she describe what she felt inside? A turmoil that had a great deal to do with Shawn Sinclair—but also something to do with his brother. The stress of the last day or two had simply been too much. If only she could just go home or at least spend some time by herself to think things over, to recover….

She couldn't. Deep inside she knew there would be no recovery for her without the truth. And only Shawn could provide that.

"I really don't want to miss the ferry, Eric."

"We still have plenty of time. Tell me, Jamie. Do you still see your father?"

She believed she knew what he was really asking. *Will my daughter survive this divorce? Will she still talk to me when she's grown?*

Jamie could have told him she was the last person to offer reassurances. But his intensity, his sincere questioning, got to her. He cared very much about that little girl.

Jamie searched for the right words. "My dad and I...we have a cordial relationship, I suppose. Not exactly close but not distant, either. Somewhere in between. He lives in Colorado. I visit him and my stepmother and my stepsisters when I get a chance. As for my mother and me...that's the more complex relationship. I see her every other day. We speak on the phone. And yet I've never told her that I love her. Mom doesn't encourage talk about such things. But, still...if you meet a man and tell *him* after four weeks that you love him, you damn well should be able to express your emotions to your own blasted family."

Jamie clenched her hands tighter, reminding herself that she usually had better rein on her tongue. She could only blame Shawn again. But perhaps she could also blame his brother. She'd just told him confidences she'd never shared with anyone else.

Not even with Shawn.

Eric drummed his fingers on the steering wheel. He didn't say a word, just stared at that old school of his.

"I want to make the ferry," Jamie said. "I need to make it."

Eric didn't speak for another long moment. Then he shrugged, as if he'd lost some argument with himself. "For what it's worth, Jamie, last night I called Shawn on his cell phone. At his number in Seattle, too. No answer."

"It was kind of you to try," she said stiffly. "But this is something I need to do myself." In the aftermath of her almost wedding, she'd already spent too much time trying to reach Shawn on his cell. Besides, what they had to discuss couldn't really be said over the phone.

Eric gave her a thoughtful look that was impossible to decipher. He reached into his pocket and took out a slip of paper. "Shawn's number in Seattle. His home address is there, too."

She smoothed out the paper and stared at it. "He never even gave me this much information. Why did he hide so much?" She'd been asking that question hopelessly. She'd never know the whys until she saw the man who'd sworn he loved her.

"What's the other address?" she asked.

"Shawn's workplace. Well, nominal workplace. He and I share management of the family firm, but he's not always a fan of clocking in."

More information she hadn't known. Jamie crumpled the paper, then smoothed it out again.

"Shawn told me he dabbled in real estate. I don't suppose *that* much is true."

"Actually, yes," Eric said.

So her intended had been truthful, up to a point. He'd told her that he was from the Northwest, that he'd grown up on the island of Saint-Anne, that he'd relocated to New Mexico because he'd always been fascinated by the Spanish architecture there.

Wasn't that the best way to lie? Be honest as far as you could. Just neglect to include certain crucial details.

"Jamie," Eric said. "For what it's worth…good luck." He gazed at her as if about to say something more. She glanced away, hoping he wouldn't say anything at all. For just a brief second she'd seen pity in his expression.

"Please," she said, her voice raw. "Let's just go."

Eric started the engine, put the truck into gear and drove her to the ferry.

Chapter Four

When Jamie reached Seattle, she had to attend to a few details. Namely she had to see about a rental car. She could not, after all, go chasing her fugitive fiancé by taxi or bus.

As she completed the necessary paperwork, the question that had plagued her ever since her arrival in Washington state surfaced yet again.

What am I doing here?

Was it sheer stubbornness? Was it as simple as refusing to accept what had happened to her at the altar? Rather too forcefully, Jamie signed her name on the rental-car agreement. As she walked across the lot and inspected the small cream sedan assigned to her, she realized her presence here wasn't as simple as the last-minute loss of a fiancé. That hurt had merely scratched the surface of a much deeper wound she held inside her.

She asked herself again, *What am I really doing here?*

A childhood memory came to her now, unbidden. That day, not long after her father had left, the snow falling thick and fast outside, unusually intense for a New Mexico winter. And Jamie, face pressed to the window, the glass cold against her cheek, straining to see through the flurry. Straining to see her dad coming up the walk, returning to her. Her mother, sitting rigidly in one of the living room chairs, pretending to read, but then, at last, setting the book down with a gesture of exasperation. "He's not coming, Jamie. He's never coming back. Accept it."

Jamie climbed into the vehicle and stared, unseeing, out the windshield for a moment. She would not—*could* not—believe that Shawn's feelings for her had been mere illusion. She would not—*could* not—make the same mistakes as her mother. Caroline Williams had never truly fought for her own happiness. Instead she had held on to her pride for almost twenty long years. But pride didn't protect you from a broken heart. It only prolonged the heartache.

Jamie turned the key in the ignition. All this time, her mother had been unable to confront the more painful dilemmas of her marriage and divorce. She'd retreated instead, as if to keep her dignity intact. But Jamie *refused* to retreat.

Pressing her foot down on the gas, she drove a little too quickly out of the lot. The rental-car company had provided her with a map and, despite the heavy traffic of the city, it didn't take her long to find Shawn's neighborhood—a tumble of exclusive homes clinging gracefully to a hillside. Shawn's house was a striking angular design, all shining glass and concrete beams. Jamie climbed out of the car, her heart thumping. She might be confronting Shawn in only a second or two.

No such luck. She stood on the porch and rang the

doorbell three times. Jamie waited for what seemed an eternity, then rang again. She waited some more. The sleek rows of windows surrounding her seemed to reflect back only emptiness.

Jamie went down the steps and turned so that she'd have a better look at the place. It was brash and elegant all at once. On the one hand, she could see the attraction. This house made a definitive, commanding statement, even while lending itself to the foliage all around. On the other hand…

It was not at all the type of home that she and Shawn had so often discussed. They'd talked about the quaint fixer-upper they'd find one day. They'd imagined spending long weekends together remodeling it or searching for antiques to furnish it. Eventually, of course, the house would be filled with the laughter and happy chaos of children—at least two. A dog to complete the picture…

This house did not seem like the type of place that would welcome children. Jamie couldn't imagine smudge prints on all those spotless windows or a bicycle sprawled on the immaculately clipped lawn. Professional gardening service, no doubt. Jamie couldn't envision Shawn pushing a mower here. Yet he'd talked about how much he enjoyed physical work, all the details of rehabilitating a home: weeding and landscaping, not to mention tearing down walls, putting up new ones, sanding and tiling and painting.

This house was too perfect. It would reject any such friendly tampering.

Jamie was more confused than ever. Shawn had

always seemed so content, so pleased to be sharing those homey, everyday dreams with her. He *couldn't* have been pretending…could he?

Jamie turned and went back to her car. She felt as if she were that child all over again, imprisoned in the house by snow. Trapped by her own inability to open the door and seek what she had lost…

If Shawn had genuinely shared her dreams, why had he left her? Why hadn't he shared *all* of his life with her? And why, dammit, had she been so blinded by love? Had she missed warning signs she might have seen otherwise?

Jamie was shaking inside. She sat in the car for a long time, gazing out the windshield. The flurry of unanswered questions tormented her. Perhaps the most insistent of all: *What am I really doing here?*

Finally, she placed her hands, which had steadied, on the wheel and pressed her foot on the gas once more.

IT OCCURRED TO ERIC that his Seattle office, of late, suffered from a split personality. A crisis of identity. It had all the necessary business accoutrements—executive desk, state-of-the-art computer, digital scanner—but one large corner had recently been converted into a play area, complete with puzzles, building blocks and stuffed animals. Taking pride of place were a long-lashed giraffe and a woolly mammoth.

Could you really run a company and at the same time compensate for having been a less-than-stellar father? Eric was trying to find out just that. He'd arranged his schedule so that he could work from home whenever possible, as well as bring Kaitlin into the office with him. He was trying to juggle everything in his life without dropping a ball. His gaze strayed toward the framed photographs displayed on his desk. Kaitlin's school portrait from last year, as well as a picture of her when she was only a few months old.

The first time Eric had held his daughter, everything had seemed possible to him. Her tiny fingers had curled around his. Odd, in a way, that such a small bundle of pink had made him feel invincible. But his child had needed him, depended on him, so of course he would be strong. Of course he would conquer the world. But even then she'd looked up at him solemnly, as if already searching the depths and complexities of their future together.

Had he begun to fail her even then? Had he spent too much time pursuing his work responsibilities and not enough time simply being her dad? Had he too often gone through the motions of being a father?

A sound at the doorway drew him from his brooding thoughts. He saw Jamie Williams framed there as if in a painting. The clear hazel of her eyes, the nuances of red and gold in her hair, the warm tone of her skin, as if a touch of sunlight had been captured there, created a palette of colors.

It hadn't been all that long since he'd seen her—he'd driven her to the ferry only this morning—but he found himself analyzing certain facets of her as if for the first time. The determined tilt of her chin, the sexy curves hinted at by that dress…

Eric rubbed his neck where that inconvenient crick seemed to have lodged of late. He reminded himself that Jamie Williams was his brother's problem.

Jamie's expressive face conveyed evident frustration. "I thought—I'd hoped, anyway…" Her voice trailed off. He knew exactly what she'd hoped: to find Shawn here.

Jamie seemed to be reordering her thoughts. She stepped into the office. "I didn't imagine you'd be here," she said. "You'd mentioned staying on the island today."

"Change of plans," he told her. "Happens more often than I'd like. Minor business emergencies. I suppose you've already been to Shawn's house."

"Yes."

"And he wasn't there."

"No, he wasn't."

"Afraid there's no sign of him here, although our receptionist tells me Shawn called to check his messages early this morning—without leaving a word about where he was…or when he would return."

Jamie appeared to tense at this information, but afterward the two of them seemed to run out of conversation. She stood halfway between the door and his desk, a slight frown on her face. Too bad Eric couldn't tell her what she needed to know, but he didn't have any insights to offer.

"Well," Jamie said at last. "It seems I'm at a dead end."

Eric went to pull out the chair on the other side of his desk. "Have a seat," he said. "And maybe…" Hell, what did he mean to say? That he'd brainstorm with her, try to think where Shawn could be? Bad idea. The best thing for her to do was go back to New Mexico and forget all about his brother.

She hesitated for a moment, but then she did sit down. Eric leaned against a corner of his desk. Jamie made a gesture that seemed to convey the futility of her situation.

"I just don't believe this," she muttered. "What do I do next—where do I go from here? Before Shawn, I always knew where I was headed. I could see tomorrow and the next day and the next. But now..."

There'd once been a time when Eric had been able to see his own way clearly. These days, however, clarity of vision was not so easy to come by.

"He has to show up sooner or later," Eric said. "He is half of this company, after all."

"You don't sound too optimistic about that."

"Shawn always has kept his own schedule," Eric had to admit. "Although he has a job title and a job description, he tends to neglect the day-to-day."

Jamie drew her eyebrows together. "Nonetheless, clearly he has responsibilities here. Why didn't he tell me any of this? What was he even doing in New Mexico?"

"Perhaps it was something of an escape."

Jamie gave him a hard look. "Escape. Why would he need that?"

He'd been mulling over certain possibilities, certain explanations for Shawn's behavior, but now he pulled back. It was useless, damaging speculation.

When he didn't answer, Jamie gave a weary shrug. "Very well, I understand. There are things you simply don't want to talk about where Shawn's concerned. But why didn't he ever tell me about his family, about his work...about his *life?*"

Why, indeed.

Eric regarded Jamie, and she seemed to grow annoyed with his scrutiny. She sat up a bit straighter.

"I can guess what you're thinking. You're trying to

figure out what I'm doing here at all. Why didn't I just stay at home and nurse my wounds in private, like a normal jilted fiancée?"

It occurred to Eric that he felt a reluctant admiration for Jamie Williams, precisely because she *hadn't* stayed at home to hide out. Clearly she was a fighter. She had courage. But that didn't change the fact that she was his brother's concern, not his.

"Jamie," Eric said, "Shawn could be anywhere right now."

"So I should just give up and go back to Albuquerque?" She gave Eric another sharp glance. "You're almost starting to look relieved. You'd like to think of me boarding a plane tomorrow, heading back to New Mexico. Another of Shawn's messes resolved—or at least out of your way."

Jamie Williams was a little too astute. He'd definitely been thinking along those lines. They looked at each other, and tension seemed to thrum between them. She was a beautiful, desirable woman who'd been mistreated by his brother. And, yes, he'd be relieved when she returned to her own life.

Just then, his daughter appeared in the doorway, her arms wrapped around a stack of file folders. When Kaitlin saw Jamie, she took a step back as if suddenly unsure. Yesterday she'd obtained a certain ease with Jamie, but that seemed to have vanished. Did she have difficulty trusting anyone these days?

"Hey there, peanut," Eric said. "Thanks for helping Mrs. Lewis with those copies."

Kaitlin nodded briefly and slid over next to him. She placed the files very carefully on the desk.

Jamie addressed Kaitlin gravely. "Why, hello there, Ms. Sinclair. I asked to speak to the president of the company, and they sent me right here to you."

Kaitlin seemed to consider this statement, but then dropped her gaze. A tough customer, his daughter.

"That's a nice outfit," Jamie went on, apparently undaunted.

Kaitlin fingered the material of her checked blue shirt.

Jamie glanced toward the corner where Kaitlin's blocks and puzzles and stuffed animals were scattered. She paused, as if debating something with herself. But then, as if she had all the time in the world, she strolled over and sat down on the floor among the toys, the skirt of her dress swirling around her. She gathered some random blocks and began stacking them one on top of the other. She didn't so much as glance at Kaitlin, behaved as if she couldn't care less whether anyone joined her.

For a minute or two Kaitlin remained right where she was, pressed against Eric's desk as if to barricade herself. But then, at last, she sat down next to Jamie on the floor, too. She gathered some blocks and began making her own stack.

Over the next several moments Eric watched the interaction between his daughter and Jamie. Anyone else might say it was almost nonexistent. Jamie seemed intent on making her own tower of blocks and didn't even glance over to look at what Kaitlin was doing. And that appeared to be exactly what Kaitlin needed. His daughter became absorbed in her own endeavor, trying to see just how high she could go.

Companionable silence. That was what the two of them were sharing.

Eric settled back, studying Jamie. She looked perfectly natural sitting on the floor next to one of Kaitlin's favorite stuffed animals—a baby cheetah. She behaved as if she had no pressing problems on her mind, no search for a wayward groom in progress. She'd come here hoping to find Shawn and instead she was entertaining Eric's daughter.

Again, *entertain* was probably not the proper term. Jamie seemed to be creating an atmosphere where his daughter could occupy herself without worry or self-consciousness. Kaitlin placed yet another block on her towering creation, then another, making her own skyscraper.

The last block was the fatal one. The whole pile toppled down as Kaitlin watched in dismay. So much for not worrying. His daughter looked as crestfallen as if she had demolished a real building.

"That," said Jamie, "was stupendous. Here—watch this." She enthusiastically sent her own tower of blocks crashing downward.

Kaitlin stifled a giggle, but not before Eric saw a trace of a smile. Undeniably, over the past several months, his daughter had grown too serious. Divorce was a serious matter, of course, but couldn't he and Leah have done more to lighten the atmosphere for their child? They'd tried to do their best, to be unfailingly polite to each other in Kaitlin's presence, to explain matters to her in clear, reassuring terms. He and Leah had also agreed that Kaitlin should see a counselor regularly to help her through this difficult transition. It had all been so well-meaning and earnest, so logical and carefully devoid of hurtful emotion. In the process, however, they'd dampened other emotions, such as simple happiness. No wonder Kaitlin tried to keep a tight rein over her feelings. She was imitating her parents.

Now Jamie and Kaitlin went back to stacking blocks, but they made a pile together this time. Jamie set one block in place, then waited as Kaitlin set her own block on top. Back and forth they went, taking turns. Another block, then another, higher and higher. Kaitlin's eyes sparkled. The pile grew and grew, becoming wonderfully precarious. And then, at last, the tower came crashing down. This time Kaitlin had to clap both hands over her mouth.

Jamie leaned toward Kaitlin. "Isn't mess fun?" she asked in a conspiratorial whisper.

Kaitlin nodded her head in agreement.

No one else might see anything of great significance happening here—just a woman and a little girl playing together—but Eric did.

Jamie Williams was special and unique. She seemed to know the secret to reaching his daughter.

In fact, Jamie Williams seemed to have something that his daughter needed.

"HELLO, MOM," JAMIE SAID, gripping her cell phone perhaps a bit too tightly. One call from her mother and all the old emotions had kicked in.

"Jamie, I knew you wouldn't find him." Caroline Williams almost sounded pleased—in her dire sort of way. Expecting the worst had become her specialty. Jamie's response was to pace back and forth in her Seattle hotel room. Eric had offered to put her up another night at his island home, but she'd decided to stay in the city. She needed solitude right now, a chance to gather her thoughts.

"I told you it was a mistake to go up there. Of course, you never listen. A letter came today, Jamie. By messenger. From *him.*"

Jamie felt herself go rigid.

"No return address," Caroline went on in a biting tone. "That's just like him, isn't it?"

Jamie tried to think of some normal, ordinary way to proceed. A letter from Shawn. The lump in her throat was so large she could hardly speak. Only with effort did she get the words out. "I suppose—if you would just forward it to me—"

"I could…if I hadn't already opened it."

That was typical Caroline Williams. Jamie supposed she ought to feel outrage at her mother's high-handed behavior, but at the moment she couldn't seem to feel anything at all. A strange numbness had enveloped her.

"I'll read it, of course." Caroline gave a discreet cough, as if about to deliver a speech. "'Dear Jamie…' Can you believe it? He leaves you at the altar and then has the gall to write you a 'Dear Jamie' letter."

"Mother."

"Yes, very well. 'Dear Jamie… You must hate me by now. You should hate me.'" Caroline Williams made a derisive sound. "Why, how kind of him. Giving us permission to despise him—"

"Mother," Jamie repeated. She sank down in the room's one armchair. "Please read it all the way through—without the commentary."

"All right." Caroline read on. "'What I've done is terrible, unconscionable. I'm sorry, Jamie, more sorry than you'll ever know. If only… Shawn.'"

Jamie closed her eyes. She'd experienced a sense of unreality listening to Shawn's words spoken in her mother's disparaging tone. *If only…* What did he mean? If only things had been different? If only he had loved her? If only they had another chance?

"That's it," said Caroline. "It's really quite masterful when you think about it. An over-the-top, extravagant apology. Gives you everything and nothing at the same time. So he takes the heat and he leaves you with nothing but coldness underneath."

Jamie considered throwing the phone across the room.

"Does he tell us *why* he left?" her mother persisted. "Does he give us *any* explanation? No, of course not. He doesn't want to be real. He doesn't want to be genuine. That would mean risking too much. Instead he gives us a smoke screen of excessive repentance—"

Jamie suspected that, in reality, her mother was no longer talking about Shawn. Caroline Williams would never admit it, but she was reliving her own pain from long ago. Jamie's predicament was no doubt forcing Caroline to confront the wounds of the past, and that could only hurt. She was lashing out in self-defense.

"I get the idea, Mom," Jamie said in a gentle voice. "I really do."

"I don't know if you really do understand," her

mother said grimly. "He left you, Jamie. He left you at the worst possible moment. And then…this letter."

Jamie sighed. Her mother never sugarcoated anything.

"I don't know anything right now, Mom. I have to think about it."

"There's nothing to think about," declared Caroline. "Come home. This is where you belong."

"I don't know where I belong anymore," Jamie said quietly. "I gave up my job. Gave up my apartment. I thought I was starting a whole new life."

"You'll stay here," Caroline insisted. "You'll stay with me."

Jamie's stomach clenched. She couldn't go back to that house, where hope and optimism were put through such a rigorous testing, they rarely survived.

"I don't know what I'm going to do," she said. "I just don't know."

A long silence from the other end of the line. And then, in a warning tone her mother said, "Make up your mind soon, Jamie. Before it's too late."

Too late? Jamie had already been hurt. She'd already been rejected. Perhaps in a way she had nothing more to lose.

If only…

Chapter Five

Eric turned the page of yet another storybook and tried to inject an appropriate growl into his voice. "'Herbert was verrry grouchy that day. He roared until he gave himself a verrry sore throat.'"

"That was good, Dad," said Kaitlin.

She'd been doing that lately, reassuring him now and then, as if she knew how hard he was searching. Looking for just the right way to be her father….

Okay, maybe he was trying too hard. Her bedtime story, for instance. He'd been operating under the assumption that if he was going to do something, he should do it right and do it all the way. If one story was good, why not two? Or three? Yet Kaitlin's eyelids were already drooping despite her best efforts to stay awake. No wonder it seemed at times that she was merely tolerating his clumsy efforts.

His daughter should be able to relax with him, not commend him for the job he was doing. And she shouldn't have to be so polite with him, so careful. Why couldn't he seem to get the balance right? What was the real secret to reaching her?

Jamie Williams, it seemed, knew at least some of the secrets.

As if sensing his thoughts, Kaitlin spoke. "Dad, why didn't Jamie stay with us tonight?"

"She's staying at a hotel in Seattle, honey."

"But it's better here. And...Isabel misses her." Kaitlin snuggled back against the pillows and held the kitten in her lap. A healthy purr emanated from the small creature.

"Jamie was only here for a visit," Eric said, searching yet again for the right words.

"Maybe...maybe she could visit again." Kaitlin stared at him steadily, intently.

"Honey, she lives in New Mexico."

Kaitlin went on with determination, as if refusing to hear him. "Maybe we could have dinner in the pool again, Dad. With Jamie. Maybe we could ask her."

How could he argue with such a simple, apparently reasonable request?

Ask her...

His daughter didn't say another word, but those serious brown eyes said it all.

Eric closed the storybook and Kaitlin nestled her head against the pillows. When he was sure that she'd gone soundly to sleep, he put the book on the bedside table. The kitten stretched its minuscule paws, yawned and settled into a deeper purr.

Eric made sure the night-light was on before switching off the lamp. He left the door wide open so that Kaitlin would be able to see the light shining from the hall if she woke.

He went downstairs and into the den, where his computer waited for the press of a button. Bringing up a spreadsheet, he tried to finish it. Working from home *did* imply working, but he couldn't seem to focus on the columns of figures. Instead his thoughts returned to his daughter.

He couldn't remember the last time she'd actually asked him for something. Yet tonight she'd made herself clear.

Please, Dad, make Jamie stay.

What could he tell his daughter? *Jamie is Uncle Shawn's problem, honey.* Kaitlin wasn't aware that Jamie was Shawn's fiancée, and there was no way Eric was going to try to explain the situation to her, either.

Eric stood and moved restlessly around the den. Gradually he noticed a new addition to the decor: a small yet dramatic clay sculpture perched on one on the shelves. As near as he could tell, it depicted the figure of a 1930s-style dancer in tuxedo and tap shoes.

On her nightly rounds the artist herself popped her head into the room. Eric had learned from experience that you didn't comment on Mrs. Braddock's artistic creations; you just allowed them to appear in unexpected places. Ever since she'd taken an art class at the Saint-Anne Community Center, she'd been a devotee of several styles. Eric hadn't minded expressionism or minimalism. He'd definitely been glad to see the end of Gothic. Art Deco, however, showed signs of promise.

Mrs. Braddock came in, picking up a stray leaf that had fallen from the azalea plant. "I suppose tomorrow's shrink day," she said in a dismissive tone. She didn't put much faith in the psychology profession. Mrs. B. had always believed in more homey remedies for heartache: a nourishing meal, a warm and cheerful house. If only those things could be enough.

"Appointment's at eleven," he confirmed. He and Kaitlin had already made several joint and individual visits to Dr. Russell. What had Eric learned so far? His daughter was having trouble coping with the divorce.

Okay, so he didn't need to pay a professional to know that much. But this particular doctor had come highly recommended by friends and she was doing her best. Eric was doing his best, too, but it still felt too damn much like going through the motions.

"Didn't quite catch that, Mrs. B."

"I didn't say anything."

"Maybe not, but you were thinking about it."

She gave him a stern glance while rattling the blinds down over the window. "Casting off and heading windward," she declared. "Ring a bell?"

As usual, he didn't have a clue what she was talking about. He waited, though, knowing there'd be more.

"Every summer since you were eight years old," said Mrs. B., "you and your grandpa would go sailing on the *Sarah Mae*. Fishing. Just drifting most of the time. There's a lot to be said for drifting."

He remembered those outings, every one of them. The sun shining on the waters of the Sound and the world beckoning. No hurry to reach any destination.

"I get the point, Mrs. B. Those experiences with Grandpa Sinclair made all the difference in my life.

Sometimes one special person in your life can make a difference…. Don't suppose you and Kaitlin have been chatting about Jamie Williams."

Mrs. B gave a too-innocent shrug and went from the room, her ponytail sailing behind her.

Eric rubbed his neck again, wondering why everyone seemed to think he had any say where Jamie Williams was concerned. First his daughter and now Mrs. Braddock.

He sat down and tried to focus on the computer screen once more but couldn't avoid the conviction that had already taken root inside him.

Jamie Williams had struck a chord with his daughter. The question, however, was what was Eric going to do about it?

KAITLIN LEANED AGAINST the ferry railing, her small face lifted to the salt breeze. Eric stood beside her, wondering once again how he would manage to juggle all the complexities of his life. A family business that these days seemed to offer more obligation than satisfaction. The dreams too long neglected. A daughter so wounded by divorce….

The idea had been, after their appointment with Dr. Russell, they would stop by his ex's house, let Kaitlin and Leah spend a little time together. Kaitlin had resisted. He'd persisted. Her eyes had brimmed with tears. End of that plan. Eric suspected Kaitlin's biggest fear was that her mother no longer loved her as she had before. If Kaitlin didn't see her mom, she wouldn't have to face even the slightest chance of rejection.

"Warm enough, sweet pea?" he asked now as they headed back to Saint-Anne after a bit of shopping.

"Yes. Thank you, Dad."

Always the formality. She was always so careful with him, so deliberate, as if working as hard as possible not to make a misstep.

Wasn't he doing the same thing these days?

Suddenly his daughter scooted closer to him. "Dad, look," she whispered. "It's Jamie."

Eric glanced over and saw a woman strolling along the deck, unmistakable red hair streaming out behind her.

"Why, you're right, peanut. It is Jamie. Do you want to go say hello?"

Kaitlin hung back, as if overcome by her own conflicting emotions. Eric held out his hand.

"We'll say hello together," he reassured her. After a second's hesitation, she slipped her hand into his.

They caught up to Jamie. She turned, her look of surprise replaced by a welcoming smile as she knelt down to Kaitlin's level.

"Hello there, Ms. Sinclair. Looks like we're both traveling the high seas today."

Kaitlin hesitated another few seconds but then answered in a soft voice, "I do this all the time."

"I'm very glad to have an expert on board. Ferries are a bit new to me. Maybe you can help me get my sea legs."

Eric studied Jamie. She wore jeans and a Windbreaker, but there was still a natural elegance about her. The breeze tangled her hair, and that hint of wild and windswept only added to her beauty.

"Dad," said Kaitlin, "is Jamie coming home with us?"

Jamie straightened and gave Eric a disconcerted look. Her skin was flushed with an appealing rose color diminished not at all by the misty gray skies overhead.

"Actually," she said, "I thought both of you knew I was coming today. Mrs. Braddock led me to understand... Anyway, she said I was invited to the island this afternoon. For tea."

Eric propped his arm on the railing beside her. "Tea," he echoed. "Let me guess. Mrs. Braddock just happened to suggest the two-o'clock ferry from Seattle to Saint-Anne."

"Why, yes. She said that would be the best one."

Mrs. B. had known, of course, that Eric and Kaitlin would be returning on the two-o'clock after their appointment with Dr. Russell and their shopping errands. She definitely had something up her sleeve.

"I wonder if we'll be having crumpets with our tea," Eric said drily.

Jamie's expressive face turned a bit more pink. "I thought meeting for tea was your idea. Mrs. Braddock all but said—"

"What's a crumpet?" asked Kaitlin.

"Well," said Jamie, "it's not quite a cake and not quite a muffin, and you eat it with lots of butter and raspberry jam."

"In the pool?" asked Kaitlin.

Eric and Jamie shared a smile.

"Perhaps," said Jamie. "Now why don't you give me a tour of this boat, Kaitlin? I want to know all about fore and aft and amidships."

Kaitlin hesitated a few seconds, but then she put her hand in Jamie's and began pulling her along.

Jamie Williams was weaving her spell again, charming his daughter. Eric could discern some elements of her magic: the way she took her time with Kaitlin, the way she behaved as if she could not possibly have anything more important to do. But there was something else, something indefinable, some essential "Jamieness" that drew Kaitlin—and he had to admit, him, as well—inexorably.

As usual, Kaitlin took her duties seriously, and it was a very thorough tour. Eric followed a few paces behind on a trek that included the auto deck, the stern, the passenger lounge and the wheelhouse. The highlight came when the captain allowed Kaitlin to place both hands on the wheel and pilot the boat. Her eyes sparkled.

Eventually the three of them returned to the passenger lounge. Eric and Jamie sat down on one of the benches while Kaitlin went to another bench across the aisle, resting on her knees so she could peer out the window.

Eric found himself speaking to Jamie in a low voice, sharing something he hadn't intended. "This morning we went into the city for our appointment with Dr. Russell, a specialist in dysfunctional families. Anyway, we had as reasonable a session as you could hope. Kaitlin tried to do a good job. My daughter even confided to me that she tried to have a breakthrough."

Jamie gazed toward Kaitlin. "I know you're very concerned about her."

"With you, Jamie, it's different. When you're around, it seems that Kaitlin doesn't have to worry about putting up a front. She can just be herself."

"Could be she's stronger than you think."

"And you, Jamie—are you stronger than you think?"

She made an impatient gesture. "I'm not sure what you're asking. I lived through my parents' divorce and I'll survive very well despite your brother—if that's what you want to know."

"Survive," Eric murmured. "Life needs to mean more than just survival." He saw the way her eyebrows drew together, as if she was lost in her own troubling thoughts. At last she swiveled toward him.

"Shawn sent me a letter, Eric. My mother read it to me over the phone last night—but I won't go into that ordeal. I just know I'm more confused than ever. 'If only,' he wrote after the requisite apology and self-deprecation. 'If only... Shawn.' What did he mean? *If only* he'd never met me? *If only* he could really explain? *If only* he could really love me? *If only* we had a second chance? What on earth am I supposed to do with that?"

They gazed at each other, not saying anything for a moment. But then Eric knew exactly what Jamie should do. The answer seemed to come to him with perfect logic and clarity, as if he'd been formulating it for a time without conscious effort.

"I have a proposition for you," he said soberly. "I'll help you get Shawn back...for the explanation he owes you. For the truth you need to discover. For the chance you still might have. I'll help you get Shawn back...if you'll help my Kaitlin smile. She knew how, once. I'd give anything to see her smile again, and something tells me, Jamie, that you're the key."

Mrs. B. hadn't made crumpets. Instead she'd served cookies and sherbet. Replete, Eric and Jamie had retired to the sun porch, while Kaitlin disappeared to help Mrs. Braddock clean up. Jamie looked as if she was getting ready to bolt. She'd reached into her purse and taken out her car keys, no doubt envisioning a rapid getaway to the docks.

Eric propped his feet on the wicker ottoman. "You still haven't given me an answer, Jamie."

She frowned at him as a delicate, alluring flush tinted her cheeks. He'd already learned that Jamie had difficulty disguising her feelings. For him it was, admittedly, a pleasant indulgence to lean back and evaluate what she was currently feeling. He detected indignation, along with a dose of impatience. Lord, she was beautiful.

Her flush deepened under his gaze.

"The whole idea is nuts," she declared. "Let's see if I have this right. I'm supposed to come stay on the island, in this very house. I'll be introduced as a 'family friend.' You'll make certain that Shawn hears about it. You have your ways and means, you say. At any rate, supposedly Shawn will learn that you and I have been seen together. He'll start to wonder, start to suspect that we may be more than 'friends.' Maybe even begin to get a little jealous. But what good is any of that really going to do?"

Eric nodded. She'd captured all the significant elements...except one. "The point is, Jamie, Shawn's a bit of a runner. He's already shown that, hasn't he? Leaving you at the altar. One way or another, he's been a runner his whole life. And the worst thing you can do to a runner is give chase. Sure, you can track him down and confront him. Sure, he might give you an explanation then. But it won't be a real one—only a deflection from his real feelings, his real self. Trust me. From my experience, if you want anything genuine from Shawn, he has to come back to you of his own accord. He needs to feel in control."

Jamie shook her head. "I just don't know," she muttered. Then she studied Eric in a skeptical manner. "Have you really thought through what we'd be getting into?"

As far as reason and logic were concerned, he'd considered every possible angle, yet he hadn't factored in certain unpredictable variables—the bemused way he felt when he was with Jamie, the way his eyes tended to linger on her, the way he liked just sitting and listening to her. Such things could get out of hand.

"Maybe," he murmured, "you're wondering if we'll play our parts too well."

She gave him a sharp look. "Is that what you're thinking?"

He was thinking about the vibrant silkiness of her hair, her creamy skin, the soft curves hinted at beneath her jeans and casual shirt. A woman as beautiful and desirable as Jamie inspired imaginative thoughts. The trick would be in controlling his imagination.

They gazed at each other for a long, tense moment. At last Jamie glanced away. "I just don't know," she repeated.

"You have to cast the bait, lure him in. Jamie, there's only one question you have to answer—do you want to resolve this or not? Are you going to let my brother get away? Are you going to let him get away with it?"

She didn't seem to have an answer to that and just continued to jiggle the keys in her hand.

"Let's face it, Jamie. If you want to get inside Shawn's head and find out why he ran—why he's still running—you'll have to make him come to you. There's no other solution. Trust me, making Shawn jealous will pique his interest and bring him back. When that happens, whether you get your explanation or get back together with him is up to you."

Jamie picked up a tropical-print cushion from the wicker love seat and turned it around in both hands. Her fingers tightened on the pillow as if she were undergoing some inner battle and the outcome remained uncertain. Was she also wondering if indeed they could go too far with this plan? Pretending an attraction when too little pretense was needed? "All I want is peace of mind," she murmured at last. "That's all. I just want some type of resolution so I can get on with my life. Dammit, it just feels that until I learn the truth, there *is* no hope of moving on."

"You can't have the truth without Shawn," he pointed out, hoping he could convince her, if only for Kaitlin. "And you can't learn the truth unless he comes to you voluntarily. He won't be able to stay away—he'll want to know if there really is anything between you and me. Shawn's competitive that way. We both are." Eric knew his brother and the logic of what he was telling her. He knew it made sense. But he also knew it was the other part of the plan that held the utmost importance for him.

Kaitlin needed Jamie. It was as simple, as irrefutable, as that. He loved his daughter. Whatever she needed, he damn well had to try and get it for her.

And so he said the words out loud. "It's a fair trade, Jamie. I'll help you with Shawn. In return, you'll help my Kaitlin."

Jamie clasped her hands on top of the pillow. "Children have a tendency to develop swift attachments," she said, as if arguing with herself. "They recover quickly, too—"

"This is different," he said.

Jamie sighed and after a long moment said, "Yes, I know."

"Yes…you'll do it?"

Her hands clenched on the pillow as if she continued to undergo that inner battle. They stared at each other again. The tension vibrated between them, a sense of unknowable dangers ahead. A sense of daring, as well. Jamie tilted her chin a bit as if meeting his challenge. She set the pillow aside.

"Perhaps I could give Kaitlin a swimming lesson or two, and if, during that time, Shawn should happen to appear…for whatever reason…"

"Ah, I see," Eric said. "You're agreeing to the ends if not the means. That'll do for now."

If they were embarking on a reckless course, it was for a good reason. He'd keep reminding himself of that.

And he'd keep trying to control his imagination.

Chapter Six

Jamie had always believed that in any endeavor, you needed to be on the lookout for hidden dangers. When you drove a vehicle, you had to scan for unexpected bumps in the road. When you flew a plane, you had to watch all indications of wind shear and turbulence. And when you had, supposedly, made a deal with your ex-fiancé's brother, you had to be alert for unintended consequences ahead.

Right now Jamie did not know precisely what those consequences would be. She just knew that she had to proceed with extreme caution. If she was going to form a friendship with one vulnerable little girl, if she was going to form a so-called partnership with the groom's all too attractive brother to inspire an appearance from the groom himself, she had to be on her toes.

At the moment, however, she was in her bare feet, studying her reflection ruefully in a boutique on Saint-Anne. She was wearing a swimsuit in bright jade-green. She'd always disliked buying swimsuits. Most women did, she knew. Something about exposing every flaw to the summer sun.

Jamie frowned at her image, feeling almost naked standing in the shop. Just then she saw Eric pacing among the racks of skirts and blouses as if seeking an escape from feminine finery. Their eyes met in the mirror. She saw the way he was looking at her. Saw the purely male appreciation as his gaze traveled over her body. Certainly he didn't seem to be searching out flaws. Then, just as quickly, the remote look returned to his eyes.

Warmth suffusing her skin, she grabbed an oversize scarf from a rack and improvised it into a sarong. Now she could turn and face him with a little dignity.

"You're blushing, Ms. Williams," he said. "Yet you don't strike me as the shy type."

First warning sign, it seemed. Her unsettling awareness of this man, one that only seemed to have intensified since they had made their agreement yesterday.

She was just feeling self-conscious, she told herself. After all, she was supposed to pretend an attraction to him. That was part of the plan. Yet somehow, as she and Eric continued to gaze at each other, she did not feel reassured.

Fortunately right then Kaitlin appeared from behind a rack of umbrellas and sun hats.

"What do you think, Kaitlin?" Jamie asked. "Is this the look we're going for?" She held up a matching swimsuit in Kaitlin's size.

The little girl's eyes seemed to shimmer. She nodded her approval. Every instinct told Jamie to go slowly and gently with Kaitlin. Nothing could be rushed or forced. If the two of them were to establish a friendship, they would need to find their way together.

Jamie was on a shopping expedition with the two Sinclairs to be on display as "the family friend"—as well as supplement the meager wardrobe she'd brought from Albuquerque. A swimsuit had been first on the list, for she intended to spend quite a bit of time with Kaitlin in the pool. When Jamie had changed back into her clothes, she came out of the dressing room and placed both swimsuits on the counter. She reached for her wallet. Eric, however, had already handed his credit card to the assistant.

"Donna," he said, "this is Jamie Williams. She's going to be staying with Kaitlin and me for a while." He'd dropped his voice ostensibly so that Kaitlin would not overhear. "Jamie is Shawn's *ex*-fiancée."

Donna leaned in confidentially, as well. "Ex-fiancée...you don't say? I didn't even *know* he had an ex-fiancée. When last I heard from him, he didn't say a thing."

The clerk made no attempt to disguise her curiosity as she completed the transaction. That was Eric's objective, of course—stir up the locals. At the next store he did the very same thing. He quietly introduced Jamie, no doubt setting up all kinds of lively speculation. Already Jamie felt like a prize exhibited at the county fair. All quite necessary, she knew, but she took refuge with Kaitlin at a jewelry counter in the next shop they visited.

"Too over-the-top?" she asked, taking a brightly beaded necklace from the rack.

"Hmm..." the little girl said.

"My thoughts exactly," Jamie agreed. She chose another necklace, this one made of small, delicate seashells, and she lowered it over Kaitlin's head.

Kaitlin nodded, solemn as ever. "Better," she said in her soft voice.

Jamie draped her own string of shells around her neck. She and Kaitlin studied their reflections in the mirror.

"What do you say?" Jamie asked. "Shall we splurge?"

Kaitlin nodded again, very deliberately.

Pretty soon Jamie forgot that she was fodder for gossip for the townspeople of Saint-Anne. She'd never known quite how much fun it could be to go shopping with a little girl. She and Kaitlin both tried on outfits, giving each other advice, while Eric waited with resigned patience. At last all three of them walked down Center Street, arms bristling with packages, but that wasn't the end of it. Kaitlin stopped to look in the door of the pet-supply shop down the way, and of course Jamie had to buy her a catnip mouse to take back to Isabel.

"You're particularly quiet, Jamie," Eric observed as they strolled down another of Saint-Anne's cobble-stoned lanes. Kaitlin had slipped ahead of them. Each time she reached one of the old-fashioned lampposts, she held on to it with one hand and circled it in her own private game. Jamie remembered the invented games of her own childhood, the ones that turned walking down an ordinary street into an adventure: looking for pennies on the sidewalk, peering into shop windows…and, yes, circling lampposts until you made yourself dizzy. If only those carefree, uncomplicated moments were the ones that would last forever.

"Are you having second thoughts?" he asked.

She gave him a sharp glance. "I never go back on a deal. But I do believe we should discuss certain pitfalls before we come upon them. For example, when the rumors start to fly about us, and Kaitlin inevitably hears…"

He seemed ready for that one. "Kaitlin will hear that you and I are friends. In reality, there won't be anything else to hear. Shawn is the one who'll wonder if there's something more than meets the eye."

"Yes, it will all be perfectly innocent," Jamie muttered. "Then why do I feel so—"

"Devious?" Eric suggested.

"Precisely."

"With Shawn, that's the way it has to be. It's all about the chase, the thrill. He'll want to know exactly what's going on between us."

She hated that. She'd always believed in being forthright and honest, in stating clearly what you wanted and then going after it. When she'd found out Shawn had kept so much from her, she knew she had to know why.

"Just trust me, Jamie."

Eric had been saying that a lot. But when she was with him, she felt as if she'd hopped aboard a speeding train and didn't know where the next stop was going to be. That intent look in his eyes, the sense that he would sweep any obstacle out of his path once he'd decided on a course of action…

She glanced away, attempting to focus on her surroundings—the quaint street with its Victorian storefronts. Beyond rose a slope of fir trees, a forest of dark green, but that view only reminded her of the murkiness of her own thoughts.

"There's something else," Jamie told Eric. "If Shawn

is off who knows where, how on earth is he going to hear about all this?"

Eric gave an unperturbed shrug. "You have to understand something about my brother. He's attached to this island in more ways than one. It's not just that we grew up here. He prefers the low-key atmosphere. One reason he neglects to show up at the Seattle office is his distaste for large projects. But on the island…it's different for him. He can find a small, struggling business that needs help. With a little investment and management expertise, he can step in and turn things around. He likes doing that—he has a talent for it. Shawn's good with people. Personal, one-on-one interaction, that's his forte."

Jamie could well believe it. The Shawn *she* knew had never considered any interchange too insignificant. When he went out to eat, he would strike up a conversation with the waiter. When he went to a movie, he'd chat with the next person in line. His interest in all the ordinary details of other people's lives was one of the things she had liked about him.

"Every store we've been in today—" Eric went on "—is one of Shawn's ventures, rescued by him in one form or another. No matter where he happens to be at a given time, he still keeps a hand in, still manages on a regular basis. He prides himself on not losing touch."

Jamie was beginning to understand quite well now. "So this little shopping expedition of ours…"

"Best broadcasting system around," Eric said with a grin. "And here's yet another of my brother's ventures." With a flourish, he opened the door of the ice cream parlor.

EVER SINCE THE PARTY days of high school Eric had understood that dancing was a whole lot more than just...dancing. Instead it was a complex ritual that encapsulated every emotion from longing to hope. The girl who turned you down after it had taken you an hour to work up your courage. The girl who finally said yes...

No, there was nothing simple about dancing. No wonder Eric had felt out of step for so long.

Tonight Eric had brought Jamie for dinner and dancing at the island's only five-star restaurant, the Harbor Bistro. The dinner part had gone fine. The dancing part...that was something else entirely.

The plan had been straightforward: a few turns around the floor, just a little something to percolate local interest about him and Jamie. He'd intended, of course, to keep her at a respectable distance—no point in overdoing the thing. But he hadn't counted on his thoughts being anything other than respectable.

She was wearing a sleeveless dress in a warm golden color. It deepened the hazel of her eyes, the red of her hair...didn't do a bad job, either, of skimming the curves of her body. There was also the matter of her perfume. Subtle, sexy... And the way she felt in his arms. That was good, too.

The lights were turned down low, the music slow and romantic. Somehow, perhaps without either of them knowing quite how it had happened, her cheek ended up against his shoulder, her sexy dress pressed against his favorite jacket and tie. He drew her just a little closer. What had his idiot brother been thinking when he left her?

The music enveloped them. He brought his fingers

up to tangle in her hair, learning the silkiness of it. What could it hurt, a moment or two? A moment of enjoying her, feeling the warmth of her, sensing deep down this was exactly what she wanted, too.

But then the music stopped and Jamie drew away abruptly. She gazed at him with an expression of dawning dismay.

"Eric..." Her voice was unsteady.

He didn't have any answer for her unspoken question. His own gaze lingered on her face, on the gentle fullness of her lips. Dancing...definitely not a simple enterprise.

The evening's mission, however, had been accomplished. As Eric and Jamie made their way toward the door, they were obliged to stop at a table here and there, introductions all around. Interest had definitely been piqued.

Eric knew there was no reason to prolong matters. He could have Jamie safely home by eleven. Say goodnight and have some time to himself to work on the Garrett buyout.

Instead, for some reason he didn't understand, he drove down Center Street, took a right and parked in front of a small office building. Unlocking the door, he ushered Jamie inside. A flick of a light switch revealed the rolltop desk that had belonged to his great-grandfather, the survey maps collected by his grandfather, the portrait of his father dominating one wall. Eric's lineage, encompassed in a space of nine hundred square feet.

"This office is where Great-Granddad started the family business," he told Jamie. "No one works here anymore, but we've kept the building as a sort of unofficial museum. A collection of relics, I guess you could say." Hearing the irony in his own voice, he opted for neutrality. "I believe he would've liked that we've held on to the remnants of those early years."

Jamie sat down in a swivel chair, vintage 1940s. She crossed her legs with the natural grace he'd been trying—unsuccessfully—to ignore all evening. No question she gave this place a touch of life and color that it had long been lacking.

Eric leaned back on a corner of the desk. "My great-grandfather started out small, buying up a project here and there. A summer cottage or two, a few acres of land."

"And now?"

The familiar restlessness took over. He stood, pacing to the wall and back again. "Now we develop commercial properties all the way from Seattle to Portland to San Francisco." He stopped in front of the window and stared out into the darkness.

"My father ran the company until nine years ago. That's when he got sick. To see him frail like that, when he'd always been so powerful... A difficult man but powerful. Anyway, someone needed to take over." Even as he spoke, Eric wondered why he had brought Jamie here. Did he really need to stir up old regrets? He'd done what was necessary to keep the family business going. In the beginning, at least, the work had engrossed him, had made him content to delay other goals for a time. The firm had grown exponentially under his stewardship. What more did he want?

Jamie turned her chair so she could study the world map above the desk. "I've always loved maps," she said.

"When I was growing up, I'd look at them and pretend that I'd be flying off somewhere for an adventure. Didn't matter where."

Her words only seemed to encourage more of that restlessness. Problem was, you couldn't pace very far in this office. Eric paused in front of the desk, rolling up the top. It opened with a protesting creak. He reached into one of the cubbyholes now revealed. A narrow scroll of paper, yellowed at the edges with age, was just where he remembered it would be.

"Great-Granddad," he murmured. "This was his first contract. He kept it to remind himself of how he'd felt when he'd taken that first step. He'd bought a fixer-upper that needed too much fixing up. Sagging foundation, rotting floorboards. Didn't matter to him, though. Day the purchase came through, he felt like the luckiest man alive." The story had become part of Sinclair family lore. How often had Eric heard it? Often enough, perhaps, to make him vow that he wouldn't let Great-Granddad down. That first step, that all-important first buy, was a legacy that continued to this day in the far-flung operations of Sinclair and Sons.

So why *didn't* Eric feel like the luckiest man alive?

Jamie was regarding him with an astute expression, as if she knew he had more to say. He returned to the window, examining the night outside as if this time it would have something new to tell him.

"Thing is," he said at last, "my great-grandfather had something I envy. Passion. He had passion for what he did. He used to say he couldn't wait to jump out of bed in the morning so he could start the day." Eric had been very young when the Sinclair patriarch had died, yet all the stories had kept the man vibrantly alive. You could almost expect the old guy to come striding through the door at any moment, wearing one of his baggy waistcoats and rolling up his sleeves so he could get down to business. He'd been as enthusiastic as any kid, even at ninety.

So was that why Eric had brought Jamie here—to tell her what was missing in his own life? She remained silent, still, and that only impelled him to go on.

"I was passionate once myself," he murmured. "Cocky, too. Got through my engineering degree in record time. I had big plans…."

And then his dad had gotten sick, and Eric had taken over the business. In so many ways, he'd done it willingly. His enthusiasm had not failed him then. He'd genuinely believed it would be possible to fulfill the family legacy and follow his own path, as well.

What had happened in the meantime?

Jamie's silence continued, her gaze thoughtful upon him. Yet there was nothing more he could say. He still had obligations to fulfill. Not to mention a daughter who needed everything he could give. This wasn't the time to open the door on abandoned dreams.

"Time to go," he said. "Sorry I kept you this long."

She went on studying him, as if searching out the answer to a puzzle. Something told him that if he took her into his arms again, he would forget those past longings and regrets. Forget them for a moment, at least.

"Time to go," he repeated, his voice rough. And Jamie didn't argue with him.

THERE WAS SOMETHING oh so satisfying about weeding a flower bed. Being on your knees, hands in the soil, yanking up those pesky little plants by their roots. Not only could you bring order and beauty to a patch of earth, you could also vent some of your frustrations. And right now Jamie had quite a few frustrations.

It wasn't Kaitlin causing this discontent. Jamie had spent an enjoyable day with Eric's daughter and their lesson in the pool had gone particularly well. If Kaitlin wasn't yet swimming in the strictest technical sense, she'd had a fine time splashing about in the water. Currently, however, Kaitlin was off in the kitchen, helping Mrs. Braddock prepare dinner, while Jamie ripped up another weed by the roots.

"Are you imagining that's me or Shawn?"

Jamie hadn't heard Eric approach behind her. She was in the back garden of the Sinclair home, where Mrs. Braddock had encouraged her to this welcome task.

Jamie stood, swiping a wayward strand of hair away from her face.

"You left some dirt behind," Eric said. His finger briefly brushed her cheek, and that alone was enough to stir more unease.

Why did she react this way whenever he was around? Why did she have to feel this awareness all through her? Especially when he still seemed to see her as a nuisance. Right now, for instance, his expression had grown shuttered, almost grim. He wore one of his well-tailored business suits, as usual giving the impression that he had more important matters on his mind.

She stepped away. "I'm almost finished. Unfortunately I didn't have all that much to do. Mrs. Braddock is far too fine a gardener."

"Mrs. Braddock said you had something on your mind."

She tossed her spade onto the grass. "It's just that...well, I only happened to mention to Mrs. B., when I was helping her empty the dishes from the dishwasher..." Jamie took a deep breath and let it all out. "Here's the thing. I quit my job, gave up my apartment, even abandoned my home state. I'm feeling completely...utterly...out of control."

"Out of control," Eric repeated with a thoughtful nod. "I understand that feeling all too well myself. My time filled with obligations, meetings, agendas, schedules. Which is worse, Jamie? No claims on your time or too many?"

She picked up her spade again. "I liked knowing where I was headed each morning. I liked driving out to the airfield and checking my schedule, knowing how many students I'd have that day. I liked the satisfaction it gave me, sharing something I loved so much with other people. I liked flying...and certainly I liked the paycheck. Now I don't know what's going to happen. I wake up in a house that's not my own and I wonder what on earth you have planned for me next." She couldn't tell him the rest of it. She couldn't confess how she'd felt when they'd danced last night and he'd held her close.

"So that's it," Eric said. "I'm the one who's making you feel out of control."

She couldn't argue with that. He was the one who'd concocted this plan, and he was carrying her along with it. Except, if she were going to be entirely honest with herself, she'd have to admit her own contribution.

Melting into his arms last night…

Eric regarded her thoughtfully. "I have an idea that might solve at least some of your problems."

When he didn't elaborate, she frowned. "Well, let's hear it."

He shook his head. "Not just yet, Jamie."

Her sense of frustration was only growing. "Why don't you tell me?"

"Everybody needs a little surprise in life." He refused to reveal any more.

"Dammit," she muttered. She knelt down and attacked another weed.

"I'm still wondering," Eric said. "Are you imagining that's me…or my brother? Which one of us is making you feel more out of control?"

Perhaps she didn't even know the answer to his question—and that scared her most of all.

Chapter Seven

Eric studied the expression on Jamie's face. She definitely didn't know how to conceal her emotions. She seemed to be wavering between surprise and chagrin.

At last she shook her head. "Mind telling me what this is all about?"

It was very early in the morning, the rose-gold of sunrise hardly faded from the sky. They were standing in the middle of Heron Airfield on Saint-Anne Island, and before them on the tarmac waited a small twin-engine turboprop. Eric was no connoisseur of planes, but a few years ago he'd availed himself of expert advice to purchase this one. He liked everything about it, from the curve of the propeller blades to the sweep of the wings and the jaunty angle of the tail. He even liked the double cobalt-blue and bright yellow racing stripe painted down the entire length of the plane. It always put him in mind of the unexpected, the unscheduled.

"Thought you could take it for a test flight," he said now.

"What's your plan this time?" Jamie asked warily.

He could tell her straight out, but somehow he didn't

think his idea would go over too well if he presented it in blunt fashion. He wanted her to warm up to it little by little. He'd considered bringing Kaitlin along for this adventure, but hadn't had the heart to wake her so early. She was at home, fast asleep under the watchful care of Mrs. Braddock. It was up to Eric alone to convince Jamie of his latest plan.

She gazed at him with suspicion. "Eric…"

"Trust me. Let's take it for a spin."

Jamie stayed right where she was. He wasn't in a hurry, though. He'd already canceled three meetings planned for today. His secretary had been in shock—he usually wasn't one for canceling.

Eric knew that he was allowing the presence of Jamie Williams to rearrange a few too many events in his life. He told himself that he had to get back on track.

Maybe tomorrow would be soon enough.

"Eric, I really wish you'd come clean."

"I'll tell you about it when we're in the air. All the arrangements have been made. She's fueled and cleared to go."

Jamie still wouldn't budge. Yet, despite her stubbornness, she appeared ready for any possibility. She wore khaki shorts, a sand-colored shirt with the sleeves rolled up and high-top hiking boots. This seemingly masculine attire failed to disguise the sexy shape of her body.

Eric frowned, running a hand through his hair.

"You have a habit of looking at me like that," Jamie said. "As if you'd temporarily forgotten my existence and I'm giving you an unpleasant reminder."

She had it all wrong. Her existence was never

possible to forget, and *unpleasant* wasn't the word he'd use. More like *disquieting* or *distracting.*

"Tell you what," he said. "Just climb inside. Have a look around."

She turned to gaze at the plane, and he read a wistfulness in her expression.

"Dammit, Eric."

He knew from the tone of her voice that he had her. Indeed, a few minutes later he and Jamie were on an inspection tour.

There was seating for six, which had always seemed just the right number—like place settings for dinner, Eric supposed. You wanted enough people to keep things lively, but you didn't want to be overwhelmed.

Jamie examined the button-back upholstery, the polished oak table tucked between two of the seats, the galley complete with foldout shelves and miniature fridge. Then she peered into one of the overhead compartments.

"Everything's in perfect condition," she said. "Someone's taken very good care here."

Jamie perched against one of the armrests. "It's uncanny. I've always had a vision in my mind of the perfect plane. And that's what this is. Absolutely perfect."

Not so difficult to understand, Eric thought. When you searched for perfection, you narrowed the field.

His gaze lingered on Jamie. After a moment or two, her face started turning that intriguing shade of pink. She glanced away purposefully.

"You're right," she said. "We should take this thing in the air, see what it's really made of."

They moved to the cockpit and Jamie seemed instantly at home, settling into her seat at the instrument panel, checking the myriad gauges. She was a natural teacher, explaining to him the displays for temperature and torque, RPMs and fuel pressure. He didn't listen to the words all that much, though. Rather, he just watched the graceful, sure touch of Jamie's hands on the controls and the way she smiled to herself.

Soon the engines roared to life, a rushing of wind magnified a hundred times. Jamie radioed the tower. She appeared completely, uncomplicatedly happy. Living in the moment, relishing it.

They taxied down the runway and waited for clearance. Then came those few seconds, always a bit startling, when the plane gathered speed, preparing to lift from the earth. Jamie seemed to give herself entirely to the skyward surge, that smile of contented absorption still playing across her face.

Eric experienced something unusual. His entire life he'd wanted to be the one in the driver's seat. He wanted to be the one in control, which was why he'd never made the best passenger. He wasn't good at sitting back and letting someone else take charge of his destiny. Yet Jamie's air of utter confidence conveyed a certainty that could not be questioned. That was what you wanted in a pilot—certainty. Conviction that no one else could do the job better. Without arrogance and without the need to say a word, Jamie had it.

She banked left and the island fell away below them. The engines gave their steady thrum, always a surprisingly relaxing sound. The color of the sky was dense, like polished opal, until the sun broke through. Then they were above the clouds, skimming the endless white.

Jamie glanced at him. That look in her eyes...yes, it was happiness. As if she never wanted to be anywhere but right here, right now. She'd found her place.

He'd felt like that once, a long time ago. He wondered if he'd ever feel that way again.

"Okay," Jamie said, "out with it."

He knew he had to choose his words strategically. "This," he said, "is the company plane. At the moment, however, I'm minus a company pilot."

He saw Jamie's hands tighten on the controls. "How about that," she said in a guarded tone. "What a coincidence. Here I am, a displaced, out-of-work pilot, and out of the blue..."

Maybe he'd jumped in too fast, hadn't given her a chance to adjust to the idea. "Yes, well...when you think about it, there's a certain symmetry here. I have a plane, no pilot. You're a pilot with no job at the moment."

"Eric, please don't tell me you fired your pilot just so—"

"Of course not," he said blandly. "Let's just say Ted had a lot of vacation time built up...and I convinced him to take it."

"You convinced him..." Jamie's voice trailed off. After a moment, she went on with an air of determination. "Eric, when I said I missed my job—I wasn't asking *you* for one. That's the last thing I'd do."

"Right. Because it would mean giving me even more control over your life, and you can't tolerate the thought of that."

She gave him an exasperated glance.

"It's just temporary," he reminded her. "Ted will use up all that vacation sooner or later. Meanwhile, this will really make Shawn sit up and take notice. You working with me…"

She drew in her breath. "Darn, I love flying. Somehow it always brings a clarity to my thoughts, my emotions…."

He gazed out at those limitless clouds. Maybe he could feel it, too. That sense of clarity. Maybe not. The way Jamie talked about flying, as if it gave her the one place in life that truly belonged to her, the one place where she felt utterly and completely at home. Undeniably he'd been drawn by that.

"What do you say, Jamie? If it's only for a short time, how much are you risking?"

She gave him a look that suggested she'd already risked too much.

"As far as Shawn's concerned, this will be the icing on the cake," he told her.

For a long while she stared straight ahead, her hands firm and steady on the controls. But then, at last, she gave a reluctant nod.

"Very well. It *is* only temporary, after all. And if it brings Shawn sooner rather than later…"

He couldn't make predictions about his own life right now, but he could get Jamie in the air again. The thought gave him pleasure. The idea that he could bring her happiness in some way—yes, that had been the deciding factor for him. He knew that perhaps he ought to analyze his own motives more carefully, but he would leave it at that. Some things would not bear close scrutiny.

THE SEATTLE OFFICES of Sinclair and Sons had captured the contrasts of the city itself. In the reception area, the pearl-gray walls evoked the northwestern sky, while the stark, modern lines of chairs and divan were cushioned in the dark forest-green so timeless to the Pacific coast. Lithographs depicted scenes in striking black and white: the graceful arches of an old stone bridge, a jumble of skyscrapers, the soaring peak of Mount Rainier.

Under other circumstances, Jamie might have enjoyed her surroundings. At the moment, however, too many emotions churned inside her. Confusion, unease…a new, unfamiliar longing that had quite a bit to do with the small hand tucked inside her own. Not to mention the ever-present unrest caused by the man walking next to her.

Eric and Kaitlin had brought Jamie to the Seattle office so she could start the paperwork as a temporary employee. The whole scheme was proceeding much quicker than she'd envisioned; they had only taken their test flight this morning. Was Eric always like this, assuming command of any situation? He took command now, introducing Jamie to the receptionist and then ushering her and Kaitlin through a warren of halls. Their progress was slow because of the employees who stopped to talk with Eric. Jamie noted his relaxed yet quietly, indisputably assured manner. No doubt he'd be the type of leader you wanted around. Someone decisive yet someone who listened to your opinion, too.

On the other hand, there were negatives about a man with such natural authority. You'd probably find yourself doing things his way almost without realizing it. Just as she had done this morning.

Eventually they arrived at Personnel, where Eric introduced Jamie and Kaitlin yet again. At least here she was the new hire—not the family friend.

"I'm leaving you two in capable hands," he said. "I'll be back soon." As he walked away, Jamie realized that both she and Kaitlin were staring after him. Disconcerted, Jamie swiveled toward the woman at the desk. Her name was Tina. She appeared to be in her midthirties and she was also very pregnant.

"Who's this?" asked Kaitlin, picking up one of the photographs from Tina's desk. It showed a little boy in a bear suit, a little girl in a pirate's outfit and a man wearing a magician's costume, cape, top hat and all.

"That's Jake, Jason and Jennifer," Tina said with a mock groan. "Jake loves Halloween almost more than the kids." She had the deprecating air of someone who knew her good fortune but did not wish to flaunt it.

"What a lovely family," Jamie could say in all sincerity. Then she turned and winked at Kaitlin. "I'll bet you like Halloween, too. What did you go as last year? A butterfly? Or a ghost?"

Kaitlin squinched up her nose. "I wore a sandwich costume," she said. "Peanut butter and jelly—Dad's favorite."

A few seconds later Jamie and Kaitlin were seated across from Tina, and Jamie's pen was poised over the requisite company paperwork. She glanced at the little girl.

"Why, Kaitlin," she said, "you're a valued employee here. Have you filled out your paperwork yet?"

Kaitlin shook her head, her eyes widening just a bit.

"It must be an oversight," Jamie said. "We'll have to correct that immediately." She'd scarcely uttered the words when Tina produced another employee packet and a freshly sharpened pencil. The woman gave a little smile as she looked from Jamie to Kaitlin and back again. Jamie could just imagine the stories that might soon be circulating around the office about the boss, the boss's young daughter and the temporary "new hire."

It would be speculation and nothing more. Jamie's relationship with Kaitlin was also temporary. There would come a time—no doubt quite soon—when she would have done all she could to help this little girl. Surely then Kaitlin would no longer need her….

The thought sent a sharp pang through her. She tried to ignore it, but it settled down into an ache that did not promise to go away anytime soon.

The two of them sat there with their company papers. Kaitlin bent over hers, writing her name very carefully in block letters. Her dark hair fell forward over her cheek. Without thinking, Jamie reached out as if to smooth the hair away. At the last second, though, she stayed her hand. She reminded herself of how gently and slowly she needed to proceed with Kaitlin. But there was something else that had stopped her. It was a warning, coming from somewhere deep inside her. *Don't get too attached….*

Was it already too late for that?

As Jamie filled in all the blanks on her form and helped Kaitlin fill in hers, the disturbing conviction would not leave her.

Perhaps it was already too late.

"THE BALLARD LOCKS were constructed almost a hundred years ago, allowing passage between Lake Washington and Puget Sound.... Tommy, for the last time, *stop* pulling Carla's hair!"

Eric, Jamie and Kaitlin observed the harried young woman shepherding a group of children, all wearing bright red T-shirts stamped Polk Community Center.

"Time-honored tradition," whispered Eric. "If you like a girl, annoy her by yanking her hair."

"Whose hair did you pull?" Jamie asked, unable to restrain her curiosity.

"Mary Ann Webster, second grade, pigtails."

"Dad!" Kaitlin said in a disbelieving tone.

"It's the truth, sweet pea. Mary Ann Webster used to get pretty exasperated with me."

"Well, I never," Kaitlin said softly.

Jamie and Eric gazed at each other. This was not the first time they'd shared a smile over something the little girl had said or done. Almost as parents might do...

Jamie propped her elbows on the railing before her and stared into the water lapping the mossy concrete walls of the channel below.

It had been only a short while since she, Eric and Kaitlin had left the offices of Sinclair and Sons. Paperwork completed, Kaitlin had requested a visit to the nearby Ballard Locks—apparently one of her favorite places. And so they had come here together, almost like a real family....

Jamie told herself yet again to stop these forbidden thoughts. She forced herself to glance around. She could see why Kaitlin liked it so much here. There was something fascinating about this place, an oasis of calm tucked deep inside the bustling city. No doubt the Ballard Locks had been a marvel of engineering when first opened in 1917. There was such a pleasing simplicity to it all: sailboats and fishing boats and kayaks jostling companionably in the smaller of the locks, the gate closing, the water lowering as if swirling out the drain of a bathtub, the opposite gate opening to beckon the way. The crews loosening their lines, joking with each other, laughter floating on the air. On the air, too, a tang of salt, a hint of the ocean.

Kaitlin wandered a short distance away, holding on to the railing as she went. Eric watched her thoughtfully. The breeze riffled his dark hair as if taunting him to let down his guard. He loosened his tie a bit yet otherwise remained the formidable businessman.

"Aren't you neglecting your work?" she asked him. "Being here with us isn't on the company agenda."

"No. Just the personal agenda."

"Because of Kaitlin," she said.

"You're good for her." He spoke somberly.

"The way you say it…it's as if you truly regret needing anything from me, Eric. This whole plan was your idea, and yet I think you really wish necessity hadn't brought us to this point."

He gave her a look that conveyed his perplexity. "Jamie, I'm her father. Shouldn't I be able to give her more?"

She couldn't answer. She'd never been a parent, so how could she offer advice?

A new contingent of boats was lining up. Beyond them, water spilled over the dam, sparkling in a shaft of light. Sun and shadow chased each other, impossible to catch. Yet everything else here was a feat of control over nature—the dam, the locks, even, as Eric had explained, a fish ladder to help the chinook and silver salmon on their perilous journeys between lake and sound.

Perhaps all control was an illusion. More than ever, Jamie did not feel in control of anything. She watched as a powerboat came into the channel. When it was securely fastened, the gates closed and the water level began to rise. The boat jostled against the walls of the lock, floating upward.

"Locking through," Eric murmured. It was a term that captured Jamie's imagination, implying as it did determination and persistence. She studied Kaitlin, who seemed engrossed in the whole process, too. The lock gates drifted open, the crew loosening the lines in readiness to cast off.

"I had so many dreams," she murmured. "Dreams I thought both Shawn and I shared. About family..." She grimaced. "White picket fence and all. Two kids, one dog. But there was even more."

Eric waited. She didn't want to go on, but she did anyway.

"Shawn and I, we were going to...start our own firm."

The skeptical look on Eric's face goaded her.

"It was all very well thought out. An air service. Executive charter, to be exact. Starting small, of course. Probably staying small, too. One special plane..." She knew all of it by heart, could have reeled off the cost-analysis figures one by one. But how could she explain the true heart of it, the excitement and adventure of such an undertaking? Especially with Eric's expression growing ever more doubtful.

"Tell me, Jamie. This white-picket-fence family stuff, was it really an idea you and Shawn came up with together? Settling down doesn't sound like Shawn."

"We talked about it all the time. Maybe I brought it up first, but still...he seemed enthusiastic." Yet, the more she considered the matter, the more it rankled. In reality, had Shawn ever actually contributed any suggestions of his own? Or had he simply listened, allowing her to talk about her hopes, behaving agreeably as if anything was possible?

Jamie turned, facing Eric, her arms folded across her chest. She felt herself tremble deep inside. "Oh, God. Did I just spin a fantasy for myself? Did Shawn ever specifically mention that he wanted a family? Maybe I just assumed it. Maybe he was just going along with what I wanted." A sense of bleakness threatened to engulf her. "If I can't even trust myself...if it was perhaps all an illusion...how will I ever have anything real?"

Eric did not seem to have an answer for her. Would she ever have *any* answers?

Jamie stared into the dark waters of the lock. Nothing seemed clear...nothing at all. Could this plan of Eric's possibly work? Would Shawn come to her—and when? What did she even expect from him—a renewal of their relationship? Or did she just want to close that door once and for all? Meanwhile, what if she was getting too attached to Kaitlin? Even worse, what if Kaitlin herself got too attached? And why did Jamie feel this constant awareness, this inescapable attraction to Eric Sinclair? When it all came down to it, what was she going to do in the end?

Chapter Eight

Mrs. Braddock popped into the den and placed a bowl on the coffee table. Eric glanced up from the Garrett papers and contemplated the housekeeper's latest creation. It looked edible enough, but appearances could be deceptive.

"Almond-chocolate-soy ice cream," she said.

Mrs. B., excellent cook that she was, liked to experiment. Eric had enjoyed the Italian-Mediterranean phase. Traditional French hadn't been bad, either—lots of crusty bread and hearty soups. But the jury was still out on California vegetarian.

"Jamie thinks it's delicious."

"Thank you, Mrs. B. I'll take it under advisement."

She gave him an astute appraisal. "Seems kind of silly to me. You down here all alone, working, with your soy ice cream. Her up there all by herself, reading, with her soy ice cream. After she read Kaitlin to sleep, of course."

Eric looked at his watch, then cursed himself. He'd missed Kaitlin's bedtime. Hadn't he sworn to himself that type of thing wouldn't happen anymore? Spending time with Jamie and Kaitlin had put him behind with his work and today he'd been playing catch-up. Ironically it was Jamie, the source of his distractions, who'd seen to his daughter.

"I suppose Kaitlin wasn't too happy with me."

"The way I understand it, Jamie kept her quite occupied. Took her to the library this afternoon, too."

Eric rubbed the crick in his neck, annoyed that he hadn't thought to do that himself, either.

"Anything else, Mrs. B.?" he asked wryly.

"Not a thing. I was just making a few observations, that's all."

Mrs. Braddock didn't ever "just" do anything. But the phone rang at that moment, and she went to answer it.

"He's right here," she said in a clipped tone, then brought the cordless to him. He didn't need to ask who it was—he could tell by the sour look on her face. Mrs. Braddock reserved that lemony expression for only one person.

"Hi, Leah," Eric said to his ex as Mrs. B. went out of the room with a disapproving swish of her ponytail.

"Hello, Eric." Cool. Remote. Unattainable. Leah had sounded that way since the moment he'd met her. She'd presented a challenge—obtaining the impossible. He hadn't yet known about all the insecurities beneath the aloofness.

"What can I do for you?"

"Please don't make it sound like I'm one of your employees and you're disappointed in me."

The crick in his neck was getting worse. "You usually don't call this late. What's up?"

"I'm concerned about our daughter. I've tried to give Kaitlin some time to adjust, but I'm her mother, after all."

They had joint custody. The arrangement between them stipulated that Kaitlin would spend the summer with him. It was understood, however, that Kaitlin could talk to Leah or visit her anytime she wished. Unfortunately, despite his best attempts to get Kaitlin to see Leah, she seemed to be retreating more and more from her mom.

"Listen," Eric said, "I should just tell Kaitlin she doesn't have a choice, she's spending the weekend with you—"

"That doesn't feel right, either. I don't want to force her. She should *want* to be with me." A significant pause. "Eric...please don't tell me that you're saying anything to her. Anything that could somehow...turn her against me."

"You know me better than that."

"Do I?" she asked quietly.

They'd been through all this before. Leah would look for any possible slight, the merest hint of criticism, and then go on the defensive. Not for the first time, Eric pondered the upbringing that had made his ex so hypersensitive. Leah's father had cared for her, but he had also seen her as a work in progress. He'd always seemed to believe that with a little effort she would be perfect. Until then, she was not quite good enough.

Eric knew about not quite measuring up. Maybe that was one of the things that had initially drawn them together.

Now he tried again. "Leah, children need direction.

Kaitlin should spend some time with you, even if she's reluctant."

"And what will that accomplish? She'll only despise me all the more."

"She doesn't despise you. She loves you, but she's afraid at the same time."

"It's complicated, I know that. You and I need to meet, Eric, and discuss this more thoroughly."

Her wanting to see him for any reason had taken him by surprise. Not so long ago, she'd declared that she'd had enough of him for several lifetimes.

He thought about it and asked the question that couldn't be avoided. "Seen Shawn lately?"

The silence on the other end of the line was potent. "I can't believe you're bringing that up again," she said in a rush. "You misunderstood everything, Eric. Perhaps deliberately."

It was kind of difficult to misinterpret your wife saying she preferred your brother. Saying, in fact, that she was in love with him.

"No, I have not seen Shawn." Another silence. Finally she said, "When will you meet me, Eric?"

They made arrangements to see each other the next day, said civil goodbyes and Eric put down the phone. He tried to return to the Garrett file, but it was no use. His concentration had vanished.

He tried a spoonful of almond-chocolate-soy. It tasted okay—maybe Jamie was right about that.

Rising, he went to the window and stared out into the darkness. He thought about Jamie, about how happy she'd been yesterday when she'd been flying. It had given him unexpected pleasure knowing that he had provided the venue for her to feel that way. He could imagine a man wanting to make Jamie feel like that all the time.

His brother had been a damn idiot in leaving her. But that didn't matter. Even though a part of Eric hoped Jamie would turn and walk away from Shawn, when he came back, she'd accept him. Women didn't easily forget his brother; his ex had already proven that. Leah denied it, but Eric knew the truth. She still wanted Shawn.

WEARING ONLY HER swimsuit, a towel wrapped around her waist and a pair of thongs, Jamie padded up the stairs of the Sinclair mansion. In the upper hallway she almost bumped right into Eric.

Startled, she retreated a step. "I didn't know you were back from Seattle," she said, oddly breathless.

"Just came in now."

"Oh...well...I just finished another swimming lesson with Kaitlin." Jamie had felt an urgent need to explain her attire, even though by now he'd seen her in this suit more than once. He wore, as usual, a flawlessly tailored business jacket, this one in smoky gray, but he tugged at his tie as if he could no longer tolerate the constraint. The more time she spent with Eric, the more she noticed the hints—the loosened tie, the dark hair worn a bit long over the collar—that his executive lifestyle did not quite fit him.

"So...how was Seattle?" Jamie asked, realizing that she sounded awkward.

He raked a hand through his hair, another clue to his restlessness. "The usual and more. I had a meeting with Leah." The words seemed to slip out against his will.

"Oh." Jamie had heard Leah's name from Mrs. Braddock. Suddenly she felt absurd. Here she stood, still damp from the pool, facing Eric the executive. She lived in his house while waiting to confront his brother, her *ex*-fiancé, and now she felt inexplicably uncomfortable talking about his *ex*-wife.

"Hope it went well," she said at last. Another inadequate comment. She intended to continue on down the hall, but Eric blocked her way.

"It hasn't gone well for some time," he muttered cryptically.

"Divorce and all…of course it must be difficult…." Why couldn't she shut up?

"Especially," he said, his voice taut, "when it seems your wife wanted your brother all along. And, apparently, he wanted her."

Jamie froze, trying to take it in. "I don't believe it," she said at last. "Shawn—he never said anything. Not even the slightest indication…" Her voice trailed off. What was the use of arguing? There was so much Shawn hadn't told her—such as the fact that he even had a brother.

And a sister-in-law.

Jamie had a cold, sick feeling inside. God, how bad *was* her judgment? Had she fallen for Shawn when he loved another woman? Not just another woman—his brother's *wife*.

The worst occurred to her. "Did they—"

"As far as I know, they didn't have an affair. I can't be sure. How the hell can you be sure of anything?"

A good question, indeed. He sounded unexpectedly weary, but Jamie was lost in her own misery.

Certain puzzling aspects of her relationship with Shawn now started to make sense. A certain perfunctory attitude at times when he expressed affection. A distant look in his eyes at other times. She'd tried to reason it all away because so often he had been warm and charming and easygoing.

And she, so captured by her own illusions, had allowed herself to be swept along.

Gradually she became aware of the intensity of Eric's gaze. All she wanted at this moment was to escape from him, nurse her shame in private. Yet he continued to block her path.

And he did something more. Unsmiling, still intense, he drew her toward him. Slowly, deliberately, his mouth descended toward hers. She remained frozen, intensely, achingly aware of his hands against the bare flesh of her back.

He was very close to her now. Closer still, and then, abruptly, before anything had really happened, it was over. Eric stepped back, his breathing as uneven as hers. He uttered a half-formed apology.

Jamie pressed her hands to her cheeks, as if that would somehow quell the blaze inside her.

"Why?" she whispered, scarcely knowing that she asked.

"I don't know why," Eric said, his voice rough. "That's the devil of it." Then he was gone from her, striding down the hall.

Jamie retreated to her room. She closed the door and leaned her forehead against it. She felt shaken to her very center. There'd been anger in that moment with

Eric, anger and despair. Had he simply been trying to blot out the memory of his ex-wife? Had she been trying to erase memories of her own?

But still something flamed inside….

Forbidden emotions swirled through her…emotions toward a man who might very well still be in love with his ex.

Maybe Shawn was in love with the woman, too. A double irony, but somehow Jamie couldn't laugh. The Sinclair brothers both wanting the same thing.

Wanting someone who wasn't Jamie.

THE NEXT AFTERNOON, Jamie pushed a cart of books between rows of shelving at the library. Eric and Kaitlin followed.

"You've been trying to avoid me," Eric remarked softly so Kaitlin would not overhear.

"Shh," Jamie muttered.

Eric now tried whispering so quietly even Jamie had difficulty hearing him. "We have to talk somewhere," he said.

Jamie didn't agree with that. Perhaps she *had* been trying to avoid him since yesterday, but she felt entirely justified. After their encounter in the hallway—after that near embrace—she'd needed time to think.

Too bad all the thinking in the world had not stilled the tumult inside her. Right now every nerve ending in her body was tautly sensitive to Eric's presence. This fact seemed to affect her coordination, causing her to drop a weighty biography of Winston Churchill.

"Got it," said Kaitlin.

Kaitlin retrieved the Churchill while Jamie and Eric gazed into each other's eyes. Jamie saw the expression of brooding discontent he reserved especially for her. If she caused him so much dissatisfaction, why had he come out of his way to see her? Today he appeared to be caught somewhere between his executive persona and his island identity. He wore a no-nonsense business shirt in cream-white, but he'd taken off his suit jacket, and his burgundy silk tie was loosened even a bit more than usual.

"Thank you, Ms. Librarian," Jamie said as Kaitlin handed the book to her. She shelved it next to a tell-all on Cicero.

"How did you find me?" she whispered to Eric.

"Mrs. B. is a fountain of information where you and my daughter are concerned. From what she told me, you two have decided to take up careers in library science."

Jamie felt the need to explain. "When Kaitlin and I were here the other day, the librarian mentioned that she was shorthanded. Kaitlin and I ended up volunteering for an hour or two. Kaitlin seemed to enjoy it so much that we volunteered again today."

Eric rubbed his jaw. "That explains why my daughter has developed a sudden interest in organizing the books on her shelves."

"It's the Dewey decimal system, Dad," added Kaitlin.

Jamie had to suppress a smile; Kaitlin had taken her new duties very seriously.

"Anyway," continued Kaitlin, "the head librarian is very friendly. Melanie's her name. She says you went to school together, Dad."

"In fact," Jamie contributed, "she was quite the fountain of information about *you.*"

Eric glanced toward the circulation desk. Melanie, a pretty blonde, instantly waved her fingers at him. She also gave him an appreciative perusal. And why not? Jamie thought. He was the type to inspire any woman's attention.

With rather more force than necessary, Jamie pushed the cart, bumping a biography of Theodore Roosevelt off a shelf.

"No problem," said Kaitlin, retrieving the volume and replacing it in its proper position. Then Kaitlin continued along the aisle, straightening books.

"Why did you come here, Eric?" whispered Jamie. "If there's something in particular you need to discuss, let's just get on with it."

To her aggravation, he wasn't in a hurry to broach the point. Instead he leaned against one of the shelves and surveyed her.

"Let me guess. Mel told you that in high school Shawn was the one with all the girls and I was the one who took life too seriously."

"Actually, she told me—" Jamie stopped herself. She didn't want to reveal what the librarian had really confessed: that Eric's intensity and unstudied virility had made him the frequent object of unrequited fantasies. Any number of girls had pined for him.

Jamie didn't want to think about it. Maybe that was the real problem—she'd been doing too much thinking altogether.

"What do you want from me, Eric?"

"I'm scheduling a trip."

She pushed her cart along. "Well, how nice for you and all. Have a good time. Don't forget to pack your toothbrush."

He remained perfectly grave. "I'll need my pilot. It's a business trip...more or less."

Jamie turned to stare at him. "More or less?"

"Actually, what if I told you this journey has nothing to do with business? What if it were entirely...a personal matter?" The words seemed to cost him, as if he'd already said too much. The worst of it was that he'd piqued her interest, which was obviously his intent.

She continued down the aisle. "Can you elaborate?"

Eric frowned at a volume of Keats. "It's just someplace I need to go. Something I need to do."

His answer was hardly enlightening, but his tone drew her interest all the more. Whatever it was seemed to mean a great deal to him.

"Where are we going, Dad?" asked Kaitlin.

"The destination I have in mind, peanut...I guess you could say it's a place I need to revisit right now. I need to see if certain perceptions still hold true."

Kaitlin seemed to give these remarks a great deal of thought. Jamie thought them over, too. Eric had shed no light on the subject, but she was, unwillingly, more intrigued than ever.

"Well," she said, "I *am* the company pilot, after all. And as long as my *copilot* is willing—" she winked at Kaitlin "—I suppose we're off to destinations unknown."

That evening, Jamie and Kaitlin spent most of their time preparing for the trip: choosing wardrobes, packing overnight bags, selecting their favorite book, their favorite toy. As Eric was working late in Seattle, they had a quiet dinner together. Jamie read Kaitlin to sleep and then spent some time with her own book, a mystery with a heroine in a strange house by the sea. At last Jamie, too, could no longer keep her eyes open.

Much later, in her dreams, Jamie was sobbing as if her heart would break. She was young—nine years old—the first winter her father had left. Her first Christmas without him. It was a season for wishes come true, and she'd wished with all her soul that he would be waiting for her by the tree. She hadn't told Mom, of course—Mom didn't believe in wishes. And so Jamie had kept her hopes to herself. But then everything was dark and she was alone, left only with her tears. It seemed that Christmas wishes didn't come true, after all….

Slowly Jamie emerged from sleep, troubled, disoriented. If it had only been a bad dream, why hadn't the crying stopped?

It wasn't just a dream.

Jamie slipped from the bed, shrugging into her robe. She nearly bumped into Eric in the hall.

"This has been happening now and then," he said, his voice taut. "This sobbing in her sleep…and then no words to tell me what's wrong. I don't know what to do."

They continued down the hall to Kaitlin's room. He rushed to his daughter's side, switching on the bedside lamp. The light fell over the two of them. Jamie couldn't see the expression on Eric's face, but she sensed his pain in the tense lines of his shoulders. She understood, felt a corresponding ache of helplessness deep inside.

Kaitlin's sobs came muffled now, her small face

pressed into the crook of Eric's arm. He smoothed the hair from her face.

"It's okay, sweet pea," he murmured. "It's okay."

And at last the crying subsided, winding down bit by bit. As if exhausted, Kaitlin nestled against the pillows, her eyelids drifting downward. Jamie watched as, very gently, Eric wiped a tear from the little girl's cheek. He waited another few moments, but it was clear now that Kaitlin slept. He switched off the lamp, leaving the hazy glow of the night-light.

Almost guiltily Jamie began to retreat down the hall. She felt like an outsider. She'd almost reached her room when she heard Eric's low voice.

"Jamie."

She turned, gathering her robe more closely about her. He stood a yard or so away, running a hand through his hair.

"She'd been doing better these last few days, since you've been here. I'd hoped these nighttime sorrows had passed."

A child crying over nameless loss. Jamie's hand went to her throat, as if she could feel her own tears there.

"I'm sorry, Eric," she murmured.

They looked at each other as if across an immeasurable distance. And then, without any more words of their own, they turned and went to their separate rooms.

Chapter Nine

Dawn had scarcely lightened the gray shadows of the sky as Jamie walked across the tarmac at Heron Airfield. The keen morning air managed to work its way through the fabric of her Windbreaker. She was already learning how changeable a northwestern summer could be, chill and warmth playing with each other in a constant game. Holding a clipboard, she scanned her preflight checklist. From long practice, she already knew each item by heart—how many times had she completed precisely this sequence?—yet each step was crucial and required her full attention. Never get complacent—that was the first rule she taught her students.

She loosened the tie-downs and removed the tire chocks on the Sinclair turboprop. Checking the fuel, examining the fuselage, the wings, the ailerons, she knew her first assessment of this plane had been correct. It had been maintained in superb condition. She ran her hand along every surface possible. A good inspection needed to be, quite literally, hands-on. You needed the feel of the plane in your very fingertips.

Enjoyably engrossed, she glanced away from her tasks only when she saw Eric's truck pull up on the other side of the fence. Eric and Kaitlin climbed out and came through the gate to the tarmac, but after that, Kaitlin hung back. It was Eric who came alone toward Jamie.

"Good morning, Ms. Williams," he remarked. "A very early morning, indeed."

"Yes, well, the company pilot is always required to get an early start."

They gazed at each other much as they had last night in the hallway, no more words forthcoming for a moment. Eric's eyes seemed an even more intense blue in this silvery light. He wore jeans and a pullover that outlined the breadth of his shoulders. If possible, he looked even more handsome than usual. Jamie had to force her eyes away from him.

She glanced toward Kaitlin. The little girl stood at a resolute distance, hands tucked firmly inside her coat pockets.

"We have a bit of a problem," Eric murmured. "Kaitlin says she's fine with flying. It's just getting on the plane that raises her objections."

Jamie was not entirely surprised. "I've been wondering if sooner or later that story of mine would have an unintended effect, telling her about my fear of planes as a child."

"Jamie, with children, you never know how something is going to have an effect. You can't blame yourself."

Despite his words, Jamie knew that Eric blamed himself quite a lot. The hazards of parenthood—guilt and worry.

Jamie strolled over to Kaitlin. "Good morning," she said casually. "Are you flying today, Ms. Sinclair?"

Kaitlin didn't say a word, but she couldn't quite seem to hide the fear in her big brown eyes.

"If you don't come along," Jamie said, "I'm not really sure how Isabel will feel."

Kaitlin gave her a speculative look this time.

"Of course," Jamie went on, "Isabel loves to fly. That's why she's already on board."

Kaitlin's gaze was suspicious now. "Isabel," she said softly, "is home with Mrs. B."

"Well, she was," Jamie admitted, "but then she wanted so very much to go on this trip with us. How could I possibly have said no?"

Kaitlin struggled with her own curiosity as Jamie turned and walked away, casual as ever. Then Jamie began climbing the steps to board the plane. At the top, she glanced over her shoulder as if in afterthought. Both Eric and Kaitlin had followed her and now stood at the bottom of the steps.

"I suppose," Eric said, "we could just take a look inside." Jamie offered her hand to Kaitlin. The little girl's fingers held tightly to hers as they climbed together into the plane. Jamie and Eric shared a quick, secret smile.

Isabel's carrier sat in the cockpit on the second's seat. Kaitlin knelt to peer in at the kitten.

"I have something of a dilemma," Jamie told the little girl. "Isabel wants very much to be the copilot today, but I'm concerned that she won't know what to do. Could you perhaps help her out just this once?"

Kaitlin still didn't say a word, but Jamie saw a sparkle in her eyes that couldn't be concealed.

So it was that a short time later all supplies and baggage had been stowed—including a generous bag of kitty chow. Jamie and Kaitlin took command of the cockpit, while Eric settled into a seat in the cabin.

"Ignition on," said Jamie.

"Check," said Kaitlin.

"Throttle closed."

"Check," said Kaitlin.

"Mixture…lean," said Jamie.

"Check."

"Flaps down, radio on."

"Check and check," said Kaitlin.

"Then…here we go."

And so, when they'd received clearance, they taxied down the runway and soon soared into the morning sky.

WHITFIELD WAS NOT A long flight. Eric's destination took them only a few hundred miles or so to this small city in the eastern portion of the state. All too soon Jamie found herself sliding out of the pilot's seat. When she was flying, she could forget her problems for a time. The sky seemed to welcome her. The air that buoyed the wings of the plane also lightened her spirits. For Jamie, the principle of lift had always been emotional as well as scientific. Because that was exactly how she felt: lifted above all problems and uncertainties.

Yet now she was earthbound once more, and nothing had been solved. Her growing confusion over Eric Sinclair. Her growing attachment and concerns for

Kaitlin. And her growing doubts about her ex-fiancé and this plan of Eric's to reel him in.

A vintage sports coupe in cherry-red awaited them. As Jamie began tucking Kaitlin and Isabel into the backseat, Eric grumbled at the sheer volume of baggage that had managed to tag along with Jamie and Kaitlin. They could hear his voice emanating from the back of the car.

"Maximum luggage…minimum trunk… What's in *this* one, bowling balls? It's only overnight, for goodness' sake. I packed less when I moved to college…."

Jamie and Kaitlin shared a long-suffering glance.

"As girls," said Jamie, "it's our prerogative to overpack." She spoke just loud enough to make sure that Eric could overhear. His head emerged at last from the trunk, his hair tousled as if he'd lost a battle with the suitcases. With an air of relief, he settled into the driver's seat and ran his hand over the steering wheel as if greeting an old friend.

"Yours?" Jamie asked as she turned to check Kaitlin's seat belt. "Where's the genie who produced this car for you?"

"We have one of our branch offices here. When I need something ready, it's provided." He spoke matter-of-factly, as if there were nothing unusual in having a luxury sports car maintained and "provided" on cue. Yet this did not jibe with his austere manner or his often relentless focus on work. Eric Sinclair was a man of contradictions, and it was the contradictions that alternately plagued and fascinated Jamie.

They swung away from the airfield, driving along a highway that led into the city.

"Last time you were here, peanut, you were only three years old," Eric said. "This part of Washington is called the Inland Empire."

It was a lofty name, but so were the mountains rising in the distance. The road took them along a wide river, the water as smooth and bright as glass just before it splashed downward over slopes of rock.

"Always liked those falls when I was a kid," said Eric. "Came here every chance I got. It's been a long while, though...." He offered nothing more, but he'd already revealed that he had a history in this place. He drove precisely along the winding road.

"I get the feeling you disapprove of this car," he said to Jamie. "No doubt you see it as an unnecessary indulgence."

"A little," she admitted. "It probably cost as much as your plane."

"I bought it right after college. It seemed to fit my life then. But now..."

"If you like something," she said, "make it fit and it's no longer an indulgence. Obviously you like this car. And you like this place, so perhaps you should come here more often."

"Nothing's that simple, Jamie." His voice held unknowable depths. The truth was, she didn't find anything simple where he was concerned.

Eventually they came to a neighborhood of shaded wandering lanes, and Eric turned down a long gravel drive. The house at the end was perfect: two-story redbrick. Not too big, not too small. Just perfect.

"It's pretty, Dad," said Kaitlin.

"Another one of my indulgences," he said almost to himself.

Eric brought the coupe to a halt on the circular drive, just in front of the house. Jamie was first out, and he tossed her a set of keys.

"You and Kaitlin have a look around while I start unloading *all* the necessities you two brought along."

Jamie and Kaitlin—and the caged Isabel—went up the porch steps. As Jamie threw the latch, Kaitlin was first through the door, her small sneakers making a pleasant echo on the hardwood floors. The house appeared to be completely empty of furnishings—a lovely shell just waiting to become a real home. All the details were gracious: oyster wainscoting, built-in bookshelves, mullioned windows with broad-plank casings.

As Kaitlin and Isabel went exploring upstairs, Eric came through the door with his first load of luggage. He glanced around reflectively.

"I bought this house with the highest of hopes," he murmured. "Unfortunately it was relegated almost immediately to…emptiness."

Jamie could not restrain herself. "What happened?"

"My divorce. I went looking for the perfect house and I found it at the most imperfect time. When a marriage starts to fall apart, there are many types of casualties. This house was one of them."

Jamie wandered from room to room and she couldn't help envisioning herself here, transforming this house into her dream home. Not too many furnishings—she'd never cared for the cluttered look. A divan here, in front of the fireplace. A floor lamp there, beside her favorite reading chair. A broadloom rug…

Eric came up behind her. "Well?" he asked.

"It's…perfect." There was simply no other word. She turned and looked at him.

"With the right person, perhaps," he murmured.

He stepped a bit closer and she couldn't look away. He brought his hand to hers and she couldn't pull back. He leaned toward her and their lips met.

Reason vanished. Nothing but sensation remained. The warmth of Eric's mouth on hers, the touch of his hand…tantalizing.

After a long, heady moment, she pulled away. Eric gazed at her, eyes darkened.

"What are we doing?" he murmured. Then he pulled her close and kissed her once more. He took her where he willed, the subtle pressure of his lips tempting her, enticing her response. Heat shimmered all through her, a cascade of pleasure and delight….

Jamie didn't know which one of them broke apart first, but her hands remained firmly planted against Eric's chest. She seemed to need propping up. It was then she heard Kaitlin's footsteps down the stairs. She and Eric stepped apart awkwardly.

"Isabel likes the room at the end of the hall, Dad."

"That's fine, peanut," he said in a distracted voice.

Had Jamie completely lost her better judgment? She had just kissed Eric Sinclair. What on earth *had* she been thinking? Yet, even now…she couldn't pull her gaze from his….

"Where's lunch?" said Kaitlin.

The picnic basket Mrs. B. had packed for them was a welcome distraction. They made a caravan out the back door: Eric with Isabel, Jamie and Kaitlin carrying the basket between them. They crossed the lawn, past a greenhouse overrun by wild roses.

"Marvelous," said Jamie almost under her breath.

They went through a gate in the weathered brick wall. A blackbird made its raspy call, and a flock of sparrows scattered overhead.

"I know you brought us here for something more than a picnic," Jamie said. "But what—"

"Patience. We'll get there soon enough."

They entered a grove of majestic ponderosa pines. Jamie wished that she could enjoy the cool green shade, but it was impossible. Eric was Shawn's *brother.* Didn't she still love Shawn despite the way he'd hurt her? If she did care for him at all, how could she be so attracted to Eric? By kissing him, she had let things go too far. Was she setting herself up to be hurt all over again?

"Relax," Eric murmured as he strolled beside her. She wondered how *he* could relax, after what had happened. She couldn't ask him in front of Kaitlin, and so the three of them walked along in silence. Apparently Eric was not concerned about the lack of words. If he didn't normally seem the picnicking type, at the moment he was giving himself admirably to the country mood. Jamie could scarcely believe that they were actually in the middle of a city, the sounds of traffic reaching them only faintly.

After a short time they emerged from the trees and came to a park along the borders of the river. A young woman lay stretched out in the grass, perusing a magazine. Two other women fast-walked along a track, arms pumping. It was all very pleasant, but the mystery remained. Why had Eric brought them here?

He led them close to the water's edge. Jamie and Eric sat down in the soft grass. This vantage point gave them an unobstructed view of the decaying stone bridge that arched across the river. After a moment Jamie recognized it as the same bridge depicted in the lithograph at Eric's office.

She lifted the checkered cloth from the basket and discovered the feast inside: a choice of almond-butter or portobello-mushroom sandwiches, tossed salad with spinach and olives, coleslaw with raisins. Mrs. B. was clearly health-conscious as well as thoughtful enough to provide vinaigrette in a separate container and ripe nectarines for dessert.

Jamie shared a sandwich with Kaitlin. Cradling the kitten in one hand and her sandwich in the other, Kaitlin went to explore the nearby playground.

Jamie studied the bridge once more. The graceful repetition of arches evoked an earlier time. She could almost imagine horse-drawn carriages rattling across or perhaps an early Model T.

Eric watched his daughter thoughtfully. "This town has grown, but it had a slow start. A hundred years ago, my great-grandfather was one of the few who saw the future here. He took some risks, bought up some land no one else wanted. Great-Granddad always said that you had to take the long view."

"And you're the trustee," Jamie murmured, "willing or not, of everything he accomplished."

Eric gave an unconvincing shrug. "It's not a bad life being caretaker of the family heritage."

"I suppose," said Jamie, "it wouldn't be bad…if it was really what you wanted."

He sat back, propping himself on one elbow. "You think I'm that dissatisfied?"

"I wonder. Are you even aware of what you feel, Eric? I suspect you've been carrying the family heritage so long you don't know how heavy it is."

He stared at that bridge, and shadows seemed to play across his face. "You're wrong, Jamie," he said in a low voice. "I remember…I remember exactly what it felt like when there was no load to carry. When I was a boy, I came to Whitfield with my granddad a lot. He was different than my father. More able to appreciate small pleasures, so he could take time out from a day's work for a grandson. We used to spend a lot of time right here. He'd tell me stories about the river, the tugboats and the barges. About the bridge, too, how it had been built when his own father was still in his teens."

Jamie watched the expression on his face, how it had relaxed for a moment.

He went on. "That's why I needed to come here today, Jamie. That bridge. When I was a kid, I always felt like it had something to tell me. And then, when I was fifteen or so, I finally knew what that something was. I wanted to build things myself—big things. Didn't seem like anything could stop me after that. When it was time for college, I set my sights on the best damn engineering program in the country, got in and relished every minute I was there."

Jamie studied his face, saw the light in his eyes and could easily imagine him fresh out of college, ready to take on the world...*his* world.

"I imagine your grandfather encouraged you," she murmured. "He sounds like someone who would."

Again Eric seemed to be gazing into the past, even as he gazed at his daughter. "Sure. Granddad told me I could do anything. And then, too quickly, he was gone. He died two months after I graduated."

"I'm sorry, Eric."

"Losing him was damn hard. But then..."

"Then your father got sick," she said quietly. "You did mention that much before."

"Yeah...he got sick. To see him like that...not in control. Frightened, even. Looking to me to make things all right, to take over the business and keep it going, when he'd never looked to me for anything before. You know one of the last things he said before he died? 'Good job, son.' I'd been waiting all my life to hear those words." The look he gave her this time was as unsmiling as ever. Intense, disturbing, sending that prickle of awareness all through her.

"But you don't really want to discuss my past, Jamie. That kiss is on your mind. Might as well talk about it. You won't feel better until you do."

"There's nothing to talk about," she said resolutely. "The kiss, unfortunately, happened. There's no taking it back." Jamie closed her eyes. She just kept remembering the feel of Eric's lips on hers.

Remembering...and wanting.

When she opened her eyes, she looked at Kaitlin in

the playground. The little girl was swinging gently back and forth with Isabel still cradled in her arms. Jamie felt a sense of protectiveness that almost made her catch her breath.

A dark-haired little girl who looked so much like her dark-haired dad....

Kaitlin left the swing and came back toward Jamie and Eric. Jamie had to blink a bit to clear her eyes as she busied herself with the picnic basket.

"Look, Kaitlin," she said, "Mrs. B. packed a surprise—oatmeal cookies." She offered one to her.

"Thank you, Jamie." Kaitlin set Isabel down, and the kitten pounced on a clump of grass as if attacking the fiercest of jungle creatures.

After that, something unexpected and wonderful and somehow entirely natural happened. Kaitlin put both arms around Jamie and gave her a big hug. Jamie's own arms tightened around the little girl as if she could never let go. She lifted her gaze to Eric's. It was impossible to tell from his grave expression what he might be thinking. But then he spoke.

"Thank you, Jamie." His voice carried a slight huskiness. "Thank you."

Chapter Ten

Jamie had always enjoyed a good campout. There was nothing quite like the crackling sound of a fire, the stars glimmering above as you snuggled against the cold in your sleeping bag.

This evening, Jamie, Eric and Kaitlin were on a campout of sorts…in the living room of the Whitfield house. Eric had thought of everything—sleeping bags, air mattresses, even the ingredients for s'mores. Logs crackled cheerfully in the fireplace. The night was warm, but a proper campout absolutely required a fire. As darkness fell, the stars sparkled beyond the windows. Kaitlin snuggled next to Jamie, and together they melted chocolate and marshmallows sandwiched inside graham crackers. Kaitlin seemed enchanted by the dance of the flames.

"Now we're cooking," Kaitlin said in her soft voice, nestling just a bit closer. Jamie and Eric shared a look by firelight. Anyone watching this scene would assume that the three of them were a family. Husband, wife, daughter.

The dangers of these thoughts. How could she be so foolish? The ideal home…the ideal family…

She knew she was already far too attached to little Kaitlin Sinclair. She could no longer deny that much. She was losing her heart to this child, losing it fast. As for Kaitlin's father…

Jamie had already made the mistake of kissing the man. And she was making the mistake of remembering. His lips on hers, his touch. She shook her head as if to free her mind, yet the memory remained, imprinted upon her. Now, as Eric gazed at her once more, she tried to blame the flush of her skin on the fire's warmth.

Kaitlin fell asleep with a smear of chocolate across her cheek. That was half the fun of camping—just this once, you could snuggle down in your sleeping bag without brushing your teeth or washing your face.

Working quietly, Jamie and Eric cleared the chocolate-bar wrappers and the half-used bag of marshmallows. They moved to the kitchen, but from here they could see through the doorway into the living room, where Kaitlin continued to sleep peacefully. "She's happy," Eric said in a low voice. "That's why she's sleeping so soundly. She was happy all day, thanks to you."

An empty pizza box and paper plates were scattered across one of the granite countertops, and Jamie was glad to have the task of gathering them up. She felt a growing tension between herself and Eric that she could not possibly explore. Keeping busy seemed the only antidote to her unease. Taking a paper towel, she wiped crumbs from the counter.

"Jamie..."

"This really is a marvelous kitchen," she said, very careful not to look at him. "Lots of space. You could have a butcher-block table there and here a rack for pans...." Somehow she wasn't helping herself. All over again she was envisioning the perfect home she'd always wanted. This kitchen had already gone a long way toward perfection: glass-fronted cabinets, walk-in pantry, tumbled-marble rose tiles along the backsplash.

Eric leaned against one of the counters, his masculinity only accentuated by these homey surroundings.

"I believe you had something of a breakthrough with Kaitlin today," he said quietly. "Since the divorce, she's been so afraid to trust. But I was right. Somehow you've got the touch. You just keep giving her what she needs, when I'm usually one step behind. And today she finally accepted that she *can* trust you." He spoke thoughtfully, with the somber air she had come to know in him. Always she sensed the questions in him, the puzzlement when it came to his daughter.

"Eric, she trusts *you.*"

"Does she? In so many ways I haven't been what she's needed. When she was younger, I gave so much energy to the family business that I neglected my own family. And then the divorce..." He glanced around restlessly. "I envisioned this house being the place where I could turn things around. I felt at home here the first minute I walked through the door. I thought Leah and Kaitlin and I could start fresh here, but it was too late. We never even had the chance to move in."

Jamie could see what he'd imagined here. This house

unquestionably deserved to be a real home, filled with love and the laughter of a child.

She dropped one of the paper plates on the floor and leaned over to pick it up. Eric bent down at the same time to help. When they straightened, they were holding the plate between them. It was a flimsy enough barrier. Eric's eyes seemed to darken as he studied her. She could feel the wild beating of her heart as she looked back at him, felt a wordless sigh escape her lips. A sigh almost of surrender…

The ringing of Eric's cell phone jolted her back to reality. He pulled his cell from the pocket of his jeans and flipped it open, raking a hand through his hair at the same time.

"Hello… Yes, Mrs. B., Kaitlin's fine. Yes, Jamie's fine. I'm fine, too. I'm sure you were about to ask…. You don't say…hmm…of course it wasn't a coincidence. He knew we wouldn't be there…. How'd he look? What's he been up to?"

Jamie tried to occupy herself again, but Eric watched her steadily the whole time this rather intriguing conversation was taking place.

"You said what to him…? No, she's right here…. And you believed him…? Of course, I have to…wouldn't you? We owe her that much."

By now Jamie had given up all pretense of not paying attention. She gazed back at Eric, listening intently to his side of the conversation.

"No, I don't know, either…. Yes, Mrs. B., the game *is* afoot. 'Bye now." Eric slipped the phone back into his pocket. "The game's afoot," he echoed drily. "Of late, Mrs. B. has been reading a little too much Conan Doyle."

At the moment, it was not Mrs. Braddock's reading habits that interested Jamie. "Mind telling me what that was all about?" she asked, barely able to contain herself.

"No, I don't mind. But you'd better sit down."

Jamie looked around. Of course, there was no place to sit in this lovely yet empty house. She folded her arms across her chest. "Please, Eric!"

"Here's the long and short of it. Shawn just happened to drop by the Saint-Anne house today. He had a little chat with Mrs. B. Shawn feigned ignorance. Mrs. B. had none of it. Shawn fished for information and Mrs. B. gave him hell."

"He showed up at the *house?*" Jamie didn't know what to feel. She was still trying to take in this information.

"The plan's working, Jamie. I told you it would."

Now she really did wish that she had someplace where she could just…sit. Since the floor was her only option, she availed herself of it, sitting down cross-legged, propping her elbows on her knees. Eric sat down across from her.

How *did* she feel? She still couldn't decide. Confusion—that was the only thing she could be certain of these days.

"I suppose," she said as calmly as possible, "you'd better start at the beginning. Where's he been?"

"It seems that after he left Albuquerque, he headed straight for California. San Diego, specifically."

"San Diego," she said irritably. "Why San Diego?"

Why? That was the question she always seemed to be asking when it came to Shawn.

"Mrs. B.'s question exactly, I believe," Eric said reflectively. "According to Shawn, San Diego is his favorite place for thinking things through."

So…Shawn had been "thinking through" the fact that he'd left her at the altar.

"Go on," she told Eric.

"It happened just as I predicted—Shawn heard that you and I had been…associating. So of course he had to come find out what the heck was going on. Trying to get information out of Mrs. B., however, backfired. She gave him a piece of her mind—a considerable piece, the way she tells it. She told him that although she loves him like a son, she hadn't done all that work helping to raise him just so he could walk out on someone terrific like you. She told him that he owes you an explanation, big-time. She told him that he'd better face up to you, double time."

Jamie took a deep breath. "And what," she asked, "did Shawn have to say to all that?"

Eric rubbed his jaw. He regarded Jamie very seriously now. "He said he couldn't see you…not just yet."

Jamie stared at Eric. "Not just yet? Dammit—" She broke off, glancing guiltily toward the living room. Fortunately Kaitlin still seemed to be sleeping soundly.

"We've got him, Jamie," Eric said. "Trust me. Now all we have to do is turn up the heat."

THE NEXT DAY AFTER returning from Whitfield, Jamie and Kaitlin were back to what had become their afternoon routine—a couple of hours' work at the Saint-

Anne library, followed by a session in the Sinclair swimming pool. The two of them never embarked on a lesson without wearing their matching swimsuits and they always invented a story for the day's lesson, pretending they were deep-sea explorers or pirates or surfers. Today they imagined they were oceanographers.

Usually Jamie welcomed any opportunity to spend time with Kaitlin. What she really wanted to do today, though, was go find Shawn and have it out with him. But Eric had said, "Trust me," yet again and had gone off to the Seattle offices of Sinclair and Sons. And Jamie found herself stewing over Shawn's visit to this very house only yesterday. She found herself mulling over his "not just yet." Worst of all, she found herself thinking about Eric…and that unfortunate kiss.

The sound of splashing water pulled her from her thoughts. "You did it, Kaitlin!" she said. "That's fantastic!"

For a brief moment the little girl really did seem to believe she'd done something worthwhile. Her dark eyes sparkled and she almost smiled.

"It wasn't really swimming," she said.

"Sure it was," Jamie countered. "You paddled your legs. You paddled your arms. That's the official definition of swimming."

"It only lasted a few seconds," Kaitlin pointed out, as precise as usual.

The two of them were in the shallow end. Kaitlin waded toward the edge, pulled herself up and sat with feet dangling in the water. Jamie went to join her. She wondered at the girl's ability to dissect and deride her own accomplishments. If only Kaitlin could simply accept the small yet brave step she'd made today.

"Let me tell you," said Jamie. "A few seconds is everything. The first flight taken by the Wright brothers only lasted twelve seconds. Yet those were the most important twelve seconds in the history of aviation."

Kaitlin appeared to consider this information, then she bent her head, toes moving back and forth in the pool. Jamie acted on a hunch.

"You know," she said conversationally, "I don't think it's the swimming that has you concerned. I think something else is bothering you."

The little girl ducked her head a bit further. Jamie moved her own feet back and forth in the water.

"Sometimes," she pushed, "it helps to talk about things with an objective party. Get a second opinion."

Kaitlin raised her head briefly. Tears glistened in the large brown eyes.

Jamie wanted nothing more than to gather Kaitlin in her arms and offer wordless comfort. She stopped herself, however. Despite the progress she'd been making with this little girl, her instincts warned her to continue treading gently, carefully. Extravagant gestures would not do the job.

"Sometimes," Jamie remarked, "other people have been through the same problems as you. They have the benefit of experience. Take, for instance, the time I was eleven and Allison Scott told everybody I had a crush on Kyle Trumbull. I was mortified—thought I could never show my face in school again. Because I really *did* have a crush on him. But then my mother gave me the best advice. She told me to act like I didn't care no matter how I felt inside. She told me to walk into the classroom with my head held up high, march right over to Allison and thank her for spreading the good news. It was the hardest thing I ever did. But you know what? It actually worked. It's no fun teasing people when you can't get them mad."

Jamie's mother had often offered good advice when it came to putting up a tough front. *Don't let your hurt show. Don't reveal weakness no matter what the cost.*

Kaitlin blinked, tears successfully averted.

"Well," said Jamie, "as for Kyle Trumbull…that didn't last long. Turns out he had an unfortunate tendency to pick his nose."

Jamie was sure she saw a hint of a smile, but it disappeared just as quickly when Kaitlin scooted back from the pool and drew her legs up. She was as changeable as the northwestern weather, clouds never too distant. Whatever was troubling her stayed firmly locked inside, her arms wrapped around her knees as if to keep any and all emotions from escaping.

It seemed that in many ways all the Sinclairs lived by the same rule: never reveal your true self. Shawn, a man she'd thought she'd known well enough to say "I love you." Young Kaitlin, always struggling to put up a brave front. And Eric, whose forbidding demeanor could serve as warning against any possible intrusion…

Jamie's gaze strayed toward Kaitlin. The little girl continued to sit there stiffly, face averted. Jamie considered the matter and came up with an idea.

"I think we've had enough swimming for today," she said. "I think now it's time for painting."

Approximately half an hour later, Jamie and Kaitlin had changed into shorts and T-shirts and were sitting at the desk in Kaitlin's room.

Isabel the cat gave a generous yawn, stretched her paws and began to purr in her basket. Kaitlin bent her head over paper and paints while Jamie picked up a brush, and her own painting began to take form: an abstract slash and swirl of vivid reds and oranges.

Jamie added another stroke of red. Art was supposed to be therapeutic. So far, she was not convinced.

After fifteen minutes or so, Kaitlin set her brush down. She inched her picture across the desk.

"You can tell me about it if you like," Jamie said very gently.

Kaitlin's brown eyes lifted mournfully. "That's me," she said, her voice so low that Jamie had to strain to catch it. "That's me...without any friends."

Jamie knew that now was the time to be as straightforward as possible. "I'm sure you have lots of friends, honey. Kids you play with at school or in the neighborhood."

"Molly used to be my friend at school," Kaitlin whispered. "She was my best friend—until she moved away."

Jamie dipped her brush in blue paint. "I know what it's like to lose your very best friend. For me, it was third grade, when Sarah Thomas moved away to Roswell. After that, I had to depend on my second best friend and my third best friend for a while. What about you, honey? Who's your second best friend? Maybe it's somebody right here on the island."

Kaitlin thought it over. "Emily," she said. And then her voice dropped again. "She was my friend *last* summer."

Jamie understood this problem, as well—summer friends. You saw each other too infrequently. Too much changed over the course of the fall and winter and spring.

"Have you tried calling Emily?"

"She's divorced, too. She's with her mom in Phoenix."

Jamie added a dab of blue to her yellow-and-red painting. Clearly action of some kind would be required in this all-important social dilemma. For now, she did her best to reassure the little girl.

"You have other friends, sweetie. You have your dad, Mrs. B. and Isabel. And…you have me."

Kaitlin studied her gravely. Then she put her arms around Jamie and gave her another hug.

Jamie hugged the little girl back. It meant so much to her that Kaitlin was opening up to her, sharing affection and confiding her thoughts. But Jamie knew, more than ever, that she was becoming attached to this child.

When the time came, would either one of them be able to let go?

IN MANY WAYS, PUGET Sound had defined the milestones of Eric's life. Whenever something important had occurred for him, those shimmering waters had played their part. His first outing with Granddad, the first time he'd stood up to his father, his first date…all had taken place on or within view of the Sound. It was therefore no accident that Eric's office provided a panoramic vista of Seattle's harbor. Sometimes he just needed to gaze at the waters. He might seek inspiration there or perspective on a problem or simply respite from a too-crowded workday.

And so, this afternoon, after the return from Whitfield, he sat in his office and stared out the window in contemplation.

"Hmm."

He hadn't heard the door open, but someone stood behind him. He didn't turn around or bother to ask who it was. He merely continued to sit there, taking in the view.

"We need to talk," said Shawn.

Eric stretched out his legs, leaned back in his chair and continued gazing. He was not surprised to hear his brother's voice. Everything was proceeding right on schedule—he'd known that sooner rather than later his brother would show up here.

"About those financials on the Garrett project," said Shawn. "Seems they're not done."

Eric watched a sailboat gliding along far below. Shawn came around the desk to face him.

"No sign of the quarterly reports, either. Since I'm fifty percent of the company, want to clue me in?"

Fifty percent was a stretch, by all accounts, given that Shawn at times used the company more as a health club than a job. But Eric wasn't in the mood for quibbling.

Shawn rooted around on the desk and found the aforementioned quarterlies. "Working capital...blank. Depreciation...blank. Current assets...blank. We haven't been burning the midnight oil on these now, have we?"

"Apparently not," Eric agreed. He knew that, deep down inside, Shawn wasn't genuinely interested in any of these business details. He'd come here to talk about

Jamie. Eventually he'd get to the point, and Eric knew confronting Shawn was never the way to go.

"Martha says you canceled the meeting with Lew Jackson at four."

"Maybe," Eric said, "you could move a little to the right.... That's better." Now he could see the sailboat again.

"Jackson's one of the best around when it comes to community development. Urban infill, compact growth, green infrastructure. We shouldn't lose a chance to collaborate with him."

"No, I suppose not," Eric said. Now he watched one of the harbor ferries inching along with its cargo of tourists.

Shawn blocked his view on purpose this time. "What gives?"

His brother looked just the same as ever—casual, elegant, sandy hair falling over his forehead, self-assured yet just the right touch of self-deprecation in his manner. Over the years Shawn had made an art of downplaying himself—understandable when your father had downplayed your abilities the entire time you were growing up.

Shawn stood there jingling the change in his pocket. It reminded Eric of when they were kids. Shawn always had been a squirmer. When their mother took them to church, five-year-old Shawn's first impulse had been to dangle upside down in the pew. He would also be the first to sprint out the door before he had to shake hands with the minister.

"It's been a while," Eric remarked.

"Yeah, well...last time I saw you, you told me to go to hell."

"Something to that effect," admitted Eric. "When you suspect your brother of having an affair with your wife, you tend to react."

Shawn paced in front of the window. "When are you going to believe me? There was never anything between Leah and me. I'd never stoop that low. Hell, we're brothers."

Eric didn't know what to believe. Leah herself had more than implied... Had she just been trying to hurt him?

Part of the problem was Shawn himself. His tactic at the moment was typical: take the defensive when he felt cornered, underline his own innocence. He'd done the same thing as a seven-year-old, when he'd been suspected of lifting change from the hall money drawer to buy comic books. He'd sworn vehemently that he hadn't done it, and Eric had backed him up—not because he was convinced by Shawn's protestations but because he suspected their father kept change in that drawer just to test them. It had seemed wildly unfair to Eric when he was nine.

How many times had he run interference between their dad and Shawn? He'd lost count a long time ago.

"You've been trying to set me up," Shawn said.

"You'll have to explain that," Eric remarked.

"You and Jamie. I hear you've been seeing her. She's ticked at me, and so are you. Payback time."

"Payback...that's a possibility. You did leave her at the altar, after all. But she's a remarkable woman. The other possibility is that I really *have* been seeing her."

What had happened between them yesterday had seemed real enough. He'd taken her into his arms. He'd kissed her. Not that he'd planned on it. He'd given in to the impulse, given himself to the moment. Jamie seemed to inspire impulses. She'd tasted soft and warm and sweet, and he'd wanted more.

A flicker of something flashed in Shawn's expression. Suspicion? Regret? It was impossible to tell.

"Anyway," Eric said, "Jamie's an amazing woman. She's unique. If you let someone like that get away, maybe you'll be kicking yourself for the rest of your life. Maybe you just have to take a chance. Maybe you have to tell her how you feel—even when you've only known her a short while."

Was he talking to Shawn or to himself?

He thought about Jamie, about her special qualities. Not just her beauty—although that was a considerable factor in her appeal. She also had warmth, decided opinions, a fierce sense of independence...a magical, nonsensical way with his daughter. She was undeniably one of a kind.

Then, quite unexpectedly, it came to Eric—the next move in this little game of cat and mouse with his brother. Of course, Jamie wouldn't like it. In fact, Eric was convinced she'd downright hate it. Still, he had promised to help Jamie get Shawn back. He'd told her that he'd be turning up the heat with his next move.

This would not only turn up the heat, it would bring everything to the boiling point.

"Shawn," he said, trying to appear convincing. "I've asked Jamie to marry me."

Shawn gave him a hard look. "No way."

"This is something I'm taking *all* the way."

Shawn continued to study him—and this time there

was definitely a flicker of uncertainty in his expression. He was clearly worried Eric just might be telling the truth.

He wasn't the only one.

Chapter Eleven

Ever since Kaitlin's revelation during their painting session this afternoon, Jamie had been brainstorming. How *did* a person, particularly a small person, go about making friends?

It was a deceptively easy question, and the answers could be all too facile, as well. Go to new places, start talking to others, be a good listener… These instructions could be daunting enough for an adult, let alone a withdrawn little girl. Added to this was the fact that every child had a different pattern for friendships. Jamie thought back to her own elementary school days. She'd known kids who had several "best buddies" at once; other children saw it as a mark of loyalty to have only one best friend at a time. She herself had fallen somewhere in between, with a small circle of two or three close friends. Jamie would have to talk to Eric, find out more about Kaitlin's past history in these matters.

Jamie caught the direction of her thoughts. She was behaving more and more as if she had a stake in Kaitlin's upbringing. Deciding she could consult with Eric the way parents consulted about their children…

Kaitlin wasn't hers. That was the stark fact. She could help, she could be a friend to this little girl, but…

Kaitlin was not hers.

Dwelling on this inescapable reality was like probing a sore tooth. And yet, this evening Eric had arranged another adventure all too reminiscent of a family outing. He and Jamie and Kaitlin were going on a bicycle tour of the island.

He'd come home early from Seattle. They'd had an early supper and now they were at one of Saint-Anne's bike-rental shops. Kaitlin had her own bicycle, of course, but Eric and Jamie needed to be outfitted.

"Dad," Kaitlin said in a long-suffering tone, "if you don't choose one soon, it'll be *midnight.*"

Eric would not be rushed. He inspected yet another bicycle critically. He'd already rejected the first three bikes. Apparently the handlebars had not been to his satisfaction, the size of the wheels inadequate. Jamie, in contrast, found the bike she liked right off the bat.

"This one'll do," she pronounced. It was an old-fashioned bike with shiny spokes and big tires, generous handlebars and a basket where you could carry your snacks. It was also sunflower-yellow. Jamie certainly wouldn't be inconspicuous, she could say that much.

Eric nodded approvingly. "I can see that you understand the importance of what we're doing here. You chose a classic."

He continued his selection process in a decided manner. "Bicycling is an art," he said. "You should appreciate it more than anyone. After all, didn't the Wright brothers start out in the cycle business? Didn't they compare flying to riding a bike?"

Jamie sighed. "You have me there. But it's been years since I rode a bike."

"They say it's one of the few things you never forget. And it's the official way to see Saint-Anne."

She'd already learned that tourists often preferred to rent bicycles for their transportation. It was, admittedly, pleasant to know you could avoid the usual crowding of cars on the island streets.

"Got it," Eric said when he'd finally made his cycling choice. A short time later the three of them were pedaling along. The breeze played with Jamie's hair, the wheels sure and steady beneath her. She realized it *was* true—you never did forget.

Eric and Kaitlin rode ahead. Ultimately he'd chosen a glossy red bike, a close match to that sports car of his. Wasn't red the color of daring and danger? Yet at the moment he kept a leisurely pace, giving Jamie the opportunity to appreciate his broad-shouldered back. She also saw the swivel of a few feminine heads as he pedaled past. No doubt it would always be this way. Eric would always attract attention, and the woman who finally won him would consider herself lucky, indeed.

Jamie swerved suddenly, almost going into the curb. Eric glanced over his shoulder.

"Okay back there?"

"Fine," she muttered. "Just fine."

He fell back to ride with her. Now Kaitlin led the

way, pedaling vigorously, her dark hair flying out from under her helmet. It was good to see her so confident.

Jamie glanced toward Eric. "I noticed you were only at the office a few hours today. Mrs. B. thinks it's a good sign that you're spending less time at work. But I'm sensing something else." Jamie downshifted as they headed up a slight incline. Eric slowed to stay with her.

"And exactly what, Ms. Williams, if you had to put it to words, are you saying?"

Jamie ignored his sardonic tone. "You're in a mood," she said. "Sort of cheerful and intense at the same time. Definitely peculiar…. Eric, has anything happened? Anything you should be telling me about?"

"We haven't exactly had a chance to talk yet, have we?" He had a knowing look on his face.

She gritted her teeth. They were having a chance right now, but clearly he was following his own agenda.

"Well, I have something to discuss with *you,*" she said. His daughter was just far enough ahead that she would not overhear. "It's about Kaitlin. Today she told me how sad she is that she doesn't have any friends. Molly's moved away, and Emily's temporarily in Phoenix. Let's see…there's also Hannah, but she's been a bit stuck-up of late, ever since she started taking ballet."

Eric's expression immediately grew grim. "I thought it would be the best thing in the world for Kaitlin spending the summer here on the island. But I didn't factor in all the variables. She hasn't spent enough time here in the past to truly be at home."

"Maybe if we put our heads together, we can come

up with some ideas." Jamie listened to herself. She was doing it all over again. Talking to Eric as if the two of them were parents, sharing all the ups and downs of raising a child together....

"Eric," she said firmly, changing the subject. "I know there's something you're not telling me. You keep saying I should trust you, but—"

"I saw Shawn today, Jamie."

Her front tire wobbled dangerously. She had to focus on the road ahead for a few minutes, before she was able to talk again.

"I'm listening," she said.

"He showed up at the office, wanted to talk about... things."

"Darn it all," Jamie exclaimed in frustration. "Mrs. B. has a chat with him. You have a chat. Well, it's about time *I* had a blasted chat—"

"Hear me out, Jamie. Shawn and I examined some what-ifs, and then I decided it was the right opportunity to make Shawn really take notice. You remember how we talked about turning up the heat—"

"Eric, are you going to tell me what's going on or not?"

"The point is, Jamie...I just happened to mention to Shawn that...you and I are engaged."

"You wha—" Jamie really did brush the curb this time and she went tumbling off the bike onto a patch of grass.

Eric and Kaitlin gathered around her with exclamations of concern.

"Jamie, are you all right?" Kaitlin asked.

"Just fine, sweetie. Just fine." She lifted her head and glared at Eric.

Kaitlin patted her arm reassuringly. "Don't worry, Jamie," she said. "You'll get the hang of it."

In spite of the bombshell Eric had just dropped, Jamie shared a smile with him over his daughter's words.

After Kaitlin and Eric helped her up and righted her cycle, Jamie started pedaling again. Several moments later Kaitlin once more sailed ahead, Jamie and Eric bringing up the rear.

"All right," Jamie said. "I'm *halfway* calm now, so explain yourself. I hope it's a very, very good explanation—"

"It is," he said imperturbably. "Shawn's smart. He knew there might be a chance we were just putting him on. Now he's not so certain. He's wondering if our relationship really is true. He's wondering if you are *my* fiancée now."

Jamie's bike almost veered again. "Eric—"

"He won't be able to stay away much longer, Jamie. You can trust me on that."

"If you say 'trust me' one more time—"

"Every part of the plan has worked so far," he reminded her. "This is just the next step. Sure, you can decide you're done with my scheme. You can go to Shawn—he's at home in Seattle now—and confront him. But you won't get the truth out of him, not unless he comes to you voluntarily. He'll have plenty to say then."

Jamie was still struggling with being "engaged" to Eric. "What's next?" she asked caustically. "A ring? Picking out china patterns together?"

"If you think that would add the proper authenticity…"

He sounded completely serious. Jamie was in more turmoil than ever and she had to find some equanimity—fast.

"Eric," she tried again. "I just wish you had consulted with me about this. It's all going way too far."

"Is it, Jamie? I have more hope about Kaitlin than I've had in months, and it's because of you."

She stared straight ahead as they pedaled over cobblestones. He seemed genuinely grateful for her help with Kaitlin and she'd been happy to give it. The other part of their plan, however, was presenting new, bewildering complications.

If anything, the situation had only become worse where Shawn was concerned. And as far as Eric himself—no answers there, no answers at all.

The three of them came to a park with wrought-iron benches surrounded by a stretch of grass. A gazebo in the very middle beckoned, and Jamie headed gratefully toward it. She and Eric sat down on the steps, while Kaitlin was drawn toward the swing set and slide a short distance away. Other children were playing there, and Jamie could only hope that Kaitlin would find a way to become part of the group. That she was making a move in that direction at all was promising.

The evening sun was putting in a last good showing after an earlier brief spurt of "beach rain." Jamie had already learned that inhabitants of the Northwest prided themselves on various categories of rain. The "beach" variety was little more than a pleasant mist, a shower of droplets that might nonetheless ebb and flow for hours.

Then, of coursc, you had the other varieties: drizzle, downpour, drenching, deluge.

Right now she was deluged by her own emotions.

Meanwhile, the ever-present fir trees helped deepen the gathering dusk. Something else about the Northwest...the greenery was always ready to envelop you in cool shade. It seemed to her that the green of this area had a special quality, something mysterious, unknowable. Rather like Eric Sinclair himself.

Eric offered his water bottle to Jamie and she took a few sips. "I don't believe it," she said, suddenly realizing the depth of her situation. "I just don't believe it. I've been dumped by one fiancé and acquired another—all in the blink of an eye."

He leaned back against the steps and gazed at her. Something in his expression sent a quiver through her.

"Don't," she said, her voice low. "Sometimes I think...well, I think that you're competing a bit too much with Shawn. And somehow...I'm in the middle."

"He's not here now. It's just you and me and Kaitlin."

"What if *she's* caught in the middle of this, too?"

"I only know that you're good for her," he said. "I couldn't ignore it, couldn't deny it. And if it's led us to this point...so be it."

"Eric, this whole thing started as an agreement. But now—I don't know what it is."

"You've kept your part of the bargain. You've spent a great deal of time with Kaitlin. I'm just trying to keep up my part. I promised to help you get Shawn back."

"Don't say it like that," she burst out. "I don't even know if I want him back. I only want the truth."

"Are you sure of that, Jamie?"

Again she found herself gazing into Eric's eyes. She saw the aloofness there but also the storminess competing.

"I'm not sure of anything anymore," she said, dismayed to find her voice trembling. She gazed resolutely toward the swings, where Kaitlin huddled by herself, apart from the other children playing there. No doubt the little girl longed to become part of the laughing, boisterous group, but she didn't know how to join in.

Just as Jamie herself didn't know what on earth to do next. She'd been engaged for real to one Sinclair brother. Was she now *falsely* engaged to the other?

ERIC WATCHED JAMIE attack the computer keys. With her red hair curling back from her face and that determined expression, she seemed to be simmering with pent-up energy.

He knew exactly what she was feeling. Against all better judgment, he studied his houseguest in greater detail. The fullness of her mouth. The dusting of freckles across her nose that, fortunately, she never tried to hide. The sandal dangling from one slender foot…

Jamie had been unusually quiet this morning, for reasons he could enumerate. One, she certainly hadn't been overly thrilled at the announcement of their "engagement." Two, she was still looking to confront her "other" fiancé. Three, Kaitlin had had another crying spell last night. Nobody in the family had gotten much sleep.

Other fragments of logic presented themselves. He'd been a damn fool to think he could kiss Jamie without changing things. She was attractive. She was desirable. Any man would have been tempted.

He was the one man who shouldn't be tempted.

What if his daughter became too attached to Jamie? What if Jamie and Shawn got back together? What if Jamie left for good? These were questions that presented no answers. He'd known only that his daughter needed Jamie and that had guided his actions. Kaitlin had undeniably thrived with Jamie's help.

And yet the questions remained.

Jamie pushed her chair away from the computer. "So much for that," she muttered.

He'd offered her free use of his computer to check her e-mail messages whenever she needed.

"You were hoping," he said, "for some emergency summons back to Albuquerque?"

She gave him a repressive look. "I'm not leaving until my *two* engagements are thoroughly resolved—no matter the difficulties."

"When it comes to difficulties," he replied, "I imagine I'm at the top of your list."

She flushed that shade of pink he liked. "Eric, you have to admit that neither one of us needs any more complications."

"Right." In theory, at least, he agreed.

"Well," she said, "nothing urgent. No emergencies. Unless you count the message from my mother telling me she *knows* what a mess I'm making of my life." Jamie headed for the door. "Thanks. Computer's all yours again."

"You don't have to leave," he said gruffly. "I heard

you tell Mrs. Braddock you wanted to start a new book. Plenty of choices in here."

"Hey, you know me—I have carte blanche at the Saint-Anne library." She hesitated, though, glancing toward the floor-to-ceiling shelves.

If he actually did have a favorite room in this house, it was the den. All the furniture here had been chosen for comfort, not style: the blocky recliner, the scarred maple desk that had enough drawers, the plain metal wastebasket he used for honing his long shot. He crumpled a sheet of paper and practiced now, missing by a good couple of inches.

"Almost, Dad." Kaitlin came into the room and around the desk to stand beside Eric. He crumpled up another piece of paper and handed it to her. She threw the ball, missing the can by a good couple of feet.

"Not bad, peanut. Try a little more wrist."

Another paper, scrunched and tossed. This one landed at Jamie's feet.

"I love basketball," said Jamie.

"Me, too," said Kaitlin.

As Kaitlin continued practicing her long shot and as Eric checked his e-mail, Jamie began examining the foldout step ladder used to reach the upper shelves.

"Wow," she said, "this is something straight out of Jane Austen. Must be quite an antique."

"It belonged to my great-great-grandmother—your great-great-great-grandmother Millie, peanut."

"That's some family tree you guys have." Jamie climbed the ladder and began perusing.

At the computer, Eric hit delete instead of send. He

could only blame Jamie for his lack of concentration. His gaze kept straying toward her. From this vantage point, he could see the hint of a tan on her legs. He could also see the curves revealed beneath her shirt when she lifted her arm to reach for another book....

She teetered a bit, trying to reach a volume on the top shelf. When he went to help steady her, her scent drifted over him. Something exotic, a combination of flower and spice. Jasmine, cinnamon...

As Kaitlin continued to practice her shot, one of the crumpled papers bounced off Jamie's shoulder. When Eric bent to retrieve it, he noticed something familiar about the crumpled ball of paper.

"Where'd you get this, Kaitlin?" he asked, smoothing out the edges.

His daughter looked guilty. The evidence was right there in front of her—she'd been rooting around in his briefcase. "I ran out of paper," she said in a small voice.

"It's okay, honey. There's more in the drawer, though."

Jamie peered over Eric's shoulder. "Hmm...looks interesting," she said.

"Not really," he said, crumpling up the paper and this time making the shot into the trash can. "Right where it belongs," he said almost to himself.

Jamie climbed down from the ladder. She advanced purposefully on the trash can and retrieved what he'd just discarded. Then she sat down on the sofa and spread the paper out on the coffee table in front of her.

"I know a blueprint when I see one," she remarked. "The legend says Whitfield Bridge. Is this the same bridge where we had our picnic?" Both she and Kaitlin regarded him with interest.

Facing both inquisitive faces, he knew there was no getting out of it. "Right after I got my engineering degree, I went to Whitfield to visit my grandfather. One look at that old bridge and suddenly I knew what my first project had to be. I was going to restore it to its former glory. So I did all the research, made the drawings, finalized the specs. I knew what a challenge it would be to preserve that bridge, make it better than new without destroying its history…."

"Let me guess," Jamie murmured. "That was about the time you took over the family business."

"That's right." He stared at the wrinkled blueprint. "It was something of a pipe dream, anyway. Better to let it go."

"Sure," Jamie said. "You've let it go. That's why you've been carrying this old blueprint in your briefcase to this very day."

Kaitlin came to stand beside him. Quite casually she put her hand on his arm and leaned over to see. "It's nice, Dad."

He put his hand over hers. "Thanks, peanut. But it really is part of the past." Kaitlin was his future. Every decision he made had to put her interests and well-being first. His needs came second. When you became a parent, you gladly changed your priorities. And so, until he could be sure that all was well with his daughter, he would put his old dreams aside.

Even dreams that refused to die.

Chapter Twelve

Kaitlin and Jamie shared a secret.

"What if he guesses?" Kaitlin asked. "What if Mrs. B. spills the beans?"

"No one," said Jamie, "can keep a secret better than Mrs. B. Don't you worry, honey. Your dad is going to be astounded."

Kaitlin's eyes shone. "He's going to be…amazed."

"He's going to be confounded…flabbergasted…thunderstruck."

Kaitlin smiled. More and more lately she was showing her emotions.

This afternoon, Jamie and Kaitlin were armed with mop, broom and dust rags. They were putting the final touches on their surprise: a transformation of the quaint, old Saint-Anne office of Sinclair and Sons.

Jamie had explained the rationale to Kaitlin. "Honey, your dad needs a place where he can remember all the plans he had when he was young."

"As young as me?"

"Just about. Your dad dreams of building things. We just have to remind him that it's okay to dream."

Jamie had come up with this idea for Kaitlin's sake as well as Eric's. Perhaps as a way to bring the two Sinclairs closer together. Yet Jamie had become just as engrossed in the plan as the little girl. She couldn't wait to see the look on Eric's face when he walked in here and saw what they had done. Why did it matter so much to her? Why did she want to get not only a smile from Kaitlin but a smile from Eric, too?

"Kaitlin," Jamie had said at last, "your father takes his responsibilities very seriously. He's worked hard to make the family business as strong and as healthy as possible. Sinclair and Sons is the family legacy…your legacy. What we want to do is help him realize there's room for more in his life."

"What's a legacy?" Kaitlin had asked. Jamie had been tempted to answer. *You are, sweetie. You're the greatest legacy of all.*

Instead she and Kaitlin had gone to the dictionary and learned all about heritage and birthright.

Now Kaitlin dusted all the cubbyholes in the rolltop desk, and Jamie swept the floor. She remembered the first time Eric had brought her to this office, only a short while ago. She'd sensed how much the place meant to him. He'd talked about having passion for your work—his great-granddad had had that, but Eric himself had lost it somehow.

Passion. Jamie understood what Eric had been talking about. She felt it when she was in the sky. It was being earthbound that gave her more than a few problems. For some reason she couldn't see all that clearly when her feet were planted firmly on the ground.

Take what was happening with Shawn, for instance. It had been days since Eric had announced their supposed engagement. The news was supposed to lure Shawn and bring him to Jamie's side so she could finally have an honest discussion with him. But so far…nothing. Not a sign of the man.

Jamie had been very tempted to take the first ferry to Seattle, march up to Shawn's door and bang on it for all she was worth. But Eric had convinced her his plan was best.

And so she focused her attention on Kaitlin. It all came back to this little girl who had worked her way into Jamie's heart. She almost couldn't imagine a life without her….

"Do you think we'll be done in time?" Kaitlin asked.

"We're just about done now. I don't think there's a speck of dust left anywhere. You've done a very good job, Ms. Sinclair."

"So have you," Kaitlin said in her soft voice. She ran to the window. "Jamie," she whispered, "he's here!"

"All right, front and center." She grabbed the dust rags, the broom and dustpan and stashed everything in the utility closet. She and Kaitlin were standing at attention by the door when Eric walked into the office.

"What's all this?" he asked. "Mrs. B. said something about an emergency."

With a flourish, Kaitlin held up the sign she had so painstakingly painted in all the colors of the rainbow. "It's Sinclair and Daughter, Dad. It's your new legacy."

The expression on Eric's face was something to see. Surprise, delight and all the love and tenderness in the world for his daughter.

"There's more, Dad!"

Like a game-show hostess, Jamie went to point out another item, this one displayed proudly on the wall among the old survey maps: Eric's engineering diploma. Mrs. B. had unearthed it from the back of a closet in the Saint-Anne house, and they'd had it framed in teak. Next to it they'd displayed a photo of Eric at his graduation, one that captured the look of purpose and enthusiasm on his face back then.

Jamie nodded at Kaitlin, giving her the prearranged cue. The little girl nodded back, then presented Eric with a scroll of paper tied in a red ribbon.

Carefully he untied the bow and unrolled the piece of parchment paper. It was more of Kaitlin's handiwork, painted in shades of blue and gold. *It's Okay to Dream,* read the scroll.

Eric looked from Kaitlin to Jamie and back again. He seemed almost too overwhelmed to speak.

Kaitlin patted his shoulder. "It's okay, Dad," she said. "It really is okay to dream."

And with that, he gathered his daughter into his arms.

Eric's reaction was all they'd hoped for, but Kaitlin wanted to make sure he'd seen every detail—how she'd straightened all the cubbies of the desk, leaving the old papers but giving him room "for your own stuff, Dad." Of course, he also had to admire the supplies she had picked out for him: the brand-new blotter on the desk, the slide rule, the T square, the cup of freshly sharpened pencils, the box of paper clips, the stack of writing pads.

When they'd all had their fill, they locked up the office and went home together for one of Mrs. B.'s wonderful dinners. In honor of the occasion, Kaitlin was allowed to stay up a little later than usual.

Eventually, however, Kaitlin was tucked into bed and Mrs. B. retired with one of her mystery novels. Eric and Jamie sat outside on the patio, candles flickering on the table between them. Nighttime cloaked them.

"It seems," Eric said, "I'm always thanking you, Jamie."

"Kaitlin and I had a wonderful time preparing the surprise for you."

"It was some surprise," he said, his voice husky.

That day in Whitfield, at the bridge park, Jamie had been captured by his enthusiasm. The way he'd talked about his college days, his dreams about building. Surely those dreams deserved to be more than castles in the sky.

Why, though, had it seemed so important to her? Why did Eric seem so important?

She had to stop this line of thinking. Kaitlin was important—of course. She had to focus only on her.

"Your daughter loves you very much, Eric, even though she doesn't quite know how to say the words. Tidying up that office, making it a place to welcome you…it mattered a great deal to her. It was a way she could show you with actions, at least, how she feels about you." Jamie shook her head. "You're not much different than Kaitlin, you know. The two of you so often try to maintain a stiff upper lip, not reveal your feelings. What's that all about?"

Even in this uncertain light she could see the sardonic expression on his face. "I guess I *have* always kept things to myself," he remarked. "Family history, I suppose. Take my mother. She was a very private woman, struggling for years to conceal how unhappy she was. She moved away from here right after my father died, back to her hometown, San Francisco. I've come to believe she was in a holding pattern the entire time she lived in Washington state. Can't blame her—my father never understood how much her own family meant to her. He expected her to bend to his ways, his life. Thing is, even when people try to conceal unhappiness, it has a way of making itself known. Maybe that's why I'm not really comfortable in this house. Too many memories of past discomfort."

"Maybe you're making new memories here," Jamie pointed out. "You and Kaitlin."

"I don't know," he said heavily. "I may have made a mistake bringing her to the island this summer. I just thought..." He made a restless gesture. "When you have a child, you plan, you organize, you think you've finally got it all figured out and then you realize you don't have anything figured at all."

The great unknowns of parenthood. Jamie could only imagine.

"Jamie, about what you did with the office—"

"I know, I know," she said. "Thank you very much—but, in reality, you see all kinds of obstacles. You've decided you can't really go off and be an engineer, not when you have a big company to run. You've revisited your dreams, but you'll keep trying to convince yourself they don't matter anymore."

"I tried being a part-time father and failed. I don't

believe in half measures anymore—for anything. But what's really bothering you, Jamie? It can't just be my pigheadedness."

She couldn't talk about it. She couldn't possibly tell him that every time she was near him, she felt drawn to him in spite of her best efforts. It was too confusing—and she was already confused enough. About Shawn. About Kaitlin. About what on earth she was going to do next with her life. And especially about Eric.

Jamie stood. "Well, it's been a busy day. No need to prolong it."

He rose and came to stand beside her in the darkness. "Prolong what, Jamie?"

"This…" She couldn't say the words, couldn't tell him that suddenly her defenses seemed to be crumbling, every part of her was achingly attuned to him.

Apparently she didn't need to tell him, though. He took her in his arms and brought her close. She felt herself trembling against him. In another second she would be truly lost. Because he would lift her face to his and he would kiss her….

"No," she whispered. "I can't. I just can't." She pushed away, turned and strode across the patio, knowing she left Eric but still hadn't saved herself.

All the longings inside her remained.

A GINGER DACHSHUND bounded across the grass, trailing its leash. A German shepherd puppy galloped behind. Meanwhile, a tabby cat had escaped into a tree and surveyed its onlookers with arrogant boredom.

"Lord," said Eric. "Is there a purpose to this madness?"

"It's only to be expected," Jamie told him. She'd convinced Eric that the Saint-Anne Community Center pet show was an excellent opportunity for Kaitlin to make new friends. Privately, though, she wondered if the chaos here might soon get out of hand.

At first, Kaitlin did not seem entirely sure of the proceedings, either. She stood close to Jamie and Eric, maintaining a tight hold on Isabel's carrier.

"Isabel doesn't like it here," she said in a clear voice. Lately she'd become much more vocal in expressing herself and that was definitely a big step forward.

Jamie knelt down beside her. "It does seem there's a lot going on, doesn't it?"

Kaitlin nodded emphatically, then glanced at Eric. "Can we go home, Dad?"

"Tell you what, peanut. We'll give it half an hour, and if you—if Isabel—still doesn't want to be here, we'll head right on home. Does that sound fair?"

Kaitlin thought about the matter, but at last she gave a reluctant nod.

Jamie straightened and scanned the chaos for any children who might make good friends for Kaitlin. The last thing she wanted to do was push Kaitlin too hard. On the other hand, a nudge in the right direction might be required here.

Jamie wished someone would nudge *her* in the right direction. She seemed to be feeling all the wrong emotions, misguided perhaps by her desire for family, her desire for home. Understandably she wanted to create the ideal family life she had never known as a child. If nothing else, she wanted to prove that the ideal *was* possible. Jamie knew, however, the peril of her own longings. All too easily she might imagine that she had found a semblance of her hopes and dreams. Despite all the commotion of the pet show, it felt so right to be here with Eric and Kaitlin. It felt as if they had truly created a real family of their own. Was that why Jamie had continued this charade of an "engagement"—she wanted to spend more and more time with Eric and his daughter, continue the illusion?

But they weren't a family, and she had to stop spinning fantasies about it. She had to remember that she'd come to Washington state so she could confront Shawn, learn the truth from him and then get on with the rest of her life.

"Relax, Jamie," Eric murmured at her side. "I know this is a madhouse, but you look as tense as Isabel."

Her gaze strayed unwillingly toward him. No business suit today, just casual slacks and one of his polo shirts. Did he realize how good he looked? Probably not—he didn't seem to be vain or overly concerned about his appearance. And that, unfortunately, made him all the more attractive. The dark hair, the strong features, always the hint of possible danger. Fall for a man like Eric Sinclair and you might never recover.

He looked back at her. Jamie's hand strayed to her throat as if to calm the pulse beating there. For a moment it seemed that only she and Eric existed, a tension thrumming between them. But then the voices of children intruded, and she came back to earth with a jolt. She swiveled away from him.

The kids seemed to be having a great time. Several

of them milled excitedly about the display tables, where dozens of ribbons waited to be awarded. There were enough ribbons, in fact, for every child to be a winner. Jamie had been happy to learn this when she'd heard about the pet show. No child would be left out today.

Kaitlin, however, was staying very close to Jamie and Eric. She held on to her cat carrier in much the same way a shipwrecked man might cling to a rock.

Jamie and Eric began chatting with some of the adults nearby, all the while shepherding Kaitlin along and giving her unobtrusive opportunities to mingle with the other children. Jamie had to admit that she and Eric worked well together, noting that eventually Kaitlin seemed much more at ease.

When they reached the refreshment table, a six-year-old boy grabbed a carrot muffin and immediately shared half of it with a black Lab. He peered into Isabel's carrier, then darted off. Meanwhile a little girl carrying a turtle in a box walked toward Kaitlin.

Jamie and Eric stepped a short distance away so they could watch without intruding. After saying hello and duly examining the turtle's spotted shell, the two children conferred intently over the cat carrier. A few moments later Kaitlin reached inside and proudly brought out the tiny Isabel. The kitten's one white paw now became a topic of lengthy conversation.

"All right," Eric told Jamie. "This has turned out to be the perfect venue for my daughter. I'm curious, though, how you came up with it."

Jamie gave a shrug. "I started thinking about those children we saw at the locks, the ones from the community center in Seattle. So I decided to check out the community center here. I figured that some type of organized activity—or disorganized, in this case—would help Kaitlin feel more comfortable. It's a chance for her to share without having to make the first move." She smiled. "For once she's not worrying about making friends and that's exactly why she's able to talk to somebody new."

"Thank you...again," Eric said.

"I wish you'd *stop* thanking me," she said, shaking her head. "I'm not doing it for that. If I spend time with Kaitlin, it's because..."

Because the little girl reminded her so much of herself as a child? Because Kaitlin needed her and it was wonderful to be needed? Because...because maybe she needed Kaitlin, too? It was the answer to that question that frightened Jamie the most.

Eric continued to regard her with a thoughtful expression. "You're making yourself indispensable," he said. "You do realize that, don't you?"

She wanted to turn away from him but couldn't. All she could do was stand there, caught in his gaze, wondering what her life could possibly be like without Kaitlin. Without him.

She struggled to remember her original goal. "There's something we need to discuss," she said at last, perhaps too forcefully, "I still haven't resolved anything with Shawn. This engagement idea of yours isn't working."

"Give it time," Eric said.

"I already have. And as far as I'm concerned, time's running out."

"So you'll go confront Shawn on your own, against all my advice. And then what, Jamie?"

"I don't know." Her throat was tight. "I just want to get everything over with so I can...dammit, I don't know."

"Seems you're about to find out," Eric murmured, looking past her shoulder. "Look who's just arrived."

She followed the direction of his gaze. None other than her ex-fiancé, her runaway groom, was coming toward her.

Chapter Thirteen

Shawn certainly knew how to make an entrance. Rather than face Jamie alone, he was leading a Scottie pup, with perky ears and bright black eyes, on a leash. Rule number one: shield yourself with an adorable companion, and your ex-fiancée—the one you'd left standing at the altar—might feel more kindly toward you.

Jamie looked Shawn over. In many ways, he was still the man she had fallen in love with. The clear blue eyes, the sandy-blond hair that fell boyishly over his forehead, the debonair manner, the understated finesse of his attire. Shawn Sinclair, for all his wealth and privilege, had never put on airs. He'd always made Jamie feel as if she were the most special and important person in the world. Come to think of it, he'd been the perfect fiancé…until he'd neglected to show up on that all-important wedding day.

He was, however, showing up now. This was the moment she'd waited for. This was why she'd come all the way to Washington state. And what was she doing with her big moment? Leaning down to pet the Scottie.

"Well, Jamie," said Shawn. "Well, Eric. This is awkward, isn't it?"

"I'll say," Eric remarked. "Whose dog did you borrow?"

"Very funny, but I'm afraid he's all mine. This new addition to my life is named McDuff." Shawn turned to Jamie and the façade slipped. A look of genuine remorse passed over his face. "I know I should have come to see you much sooner. I've thought about you, Jamie—little else, in fact. I'm here," he said, "to face the music. I messed up and I know it."

"I've already had your letter of apology," she remarked. "I was expecting something a little more substantial." She'd asked herself many times how she would feel when she finally saw Shawn again and had speculated about all the possible reactions: anger, hurt, indignation. What she didn't expect was to feel all of those at once.

"I'm here to talk," Shawn said quietly. "I really am."

Jamie glanced from one brother to the other. They were undeniably different—one of them fair, the other dark-haired—and yet the similarities could not be denied, either. Both Eric and Shawn shared a particular assessing way of gazing at the world, a self-assurance that *did* come from a life of privilege. They also seemed to be taking each other's measure, as if from long practice.

"Eric," Jamie said, "if you'll excuse us, Shawn and I are going to…have a talk."

"Sure thing, dear," said Eric.

Oh, damn. Jamie had almost forgotten that she and Eric were supposedly *engaged.* She gave him a quelling look that seemed to have no effect whatsoever.

Without asking, he took the leash from Shawn and began walking away. "I'll just introduce McDuff to your niece, Shawn," he said over his shoulder. "And Jamie...I'm here if you need me." He really seemed to mean it.

Purposefully Jamie led Shawn into the community center's gym. Despite the chaos of the day, this particular area was not in use.

Shawn took hold of a basketball and bounced it once or twice. He'd finally come to see her—he was finally facing up to her—but he didn't seem to know how to begin. He bounced the ball a few more times, frowning at it. Jamie considered jump-starting the difficult conversation ahead but then decided against it. Shawn was the one who had to explain himself—not the other way around.

At last Shawn set down the ball. "I'm sorry, Jamie," he said in a low voice.

She shrugged. "You've already told me that. First in your phone message and then your letter."

"I can't say it enough." He regarded her. "It would be better if you blamed me. I know I deserve it."

"Believe me, Shawn," she remarked, "I *do* blame you."

He ran a hand through his hair in a gesture that reminded her of Eric. He seemed to be searching for a new tack. "You can level with me, Jamie. If you and Eric are trying to make me jealous, it's worked. You don't have to put up any more pretense."

She felt another surge of anger. "This is about you and me, Shawn."

He gave her a speculative look, as if trying to sort out

the truth about her and his brother. Yet *he* was the one who needed to be sharing truths right now.

Jamie was getting more impatient. Time for a new tactic. Not accusations—just a simple question.

"Shawn, what were you running from when you came to New Mexico?"

"I wasn't running," he said, perhaps a bit too quickly.

"I don't believe you," she said. "Maybe I was a consolation prize, nothing more. Maybe that's why you couldn't show up at the church. I wasn't what you really wanted."

He sighed. "You're talking about Leah, aren't you? I guess my brother told you all about it—except there's nothing to tell. I didn't have an affair with her, Jamie. It's true that she depended on me for a while when… when things started to go bad between her and Eric. She just needed me as a friend, that's all. Never anything else. Tell me you believe that much."

She didn't know what to believe—that was the whole problem. "I'm listening," she said in a restrained tone.

"You were everything I wanted," he told her. "It's just…I was afraid I couldn't be what *you* really needed. I didn't want to leave you, though. Right up until zero hour, I intended to go through with it."

That was too much, and Jamie could no longer contain her indignation. "Listen to yourself. *Zero hour. Go through with it.* Doesn't your choice of words tell you anything?" Now she was the one who took the basketball and gave it an emphatic bounce. "When you find something you're sure is perfect, you don't stop to question it. You just grab on and you don't let go. That's what I did, Shawn. It was foolhardy, it was stupid, but at least it was honest. That's not what happened with you, though. You were just going through the motions the whole time with me. Saying the things I wanted to hear, being the person I wanted you to be. The real you never made an appearance."

"That's not true, Jamie—"

"Isn't it?"

They stared at each other. And then Shawn sat down on one of the bleachers, almost with a gesture of defeat.

"All right, Jamie, I'll tell you everything I can. When I came to New Mexico, I was trying to get away. I was confused about my feelings for Leah. *Not* that we had an affair," he reiterated. "I wouldn't do that to my own brother. But I had to leave, had to get away. Then I met you, Jamie, and things started to get really complicated."

Jamie sat down next to him. "Go on."

The old endearing smile played over his face. "The truth is, you were exactly what I've always wanted in a woman. I think that's what scared me. To find the perfect situation, the perfect woman…all seemed too good to be true. What if I ruined it? What if I failed you? What if, when you really came to know me, you were disappointed? All those things ran through my mind, Jamie. It's never easy to look inside yourself. And so, at the last minute…I didn't come through for you. I'll always regret not showing up at the church. I'll regret it more than anything."

There was something different about Shawn now, a quality she hadn't seen in him before. His demeanor was entirely new, the boyish charm dropping away. She was convinced he was finally being real with her. She looked into his eyes and saw the sincerity there...and the sadness. But there was still one piece of the puzzle missing—the most important piece.

"I understand about being afraid," she said. "I understand about not being able to take the last, final step because you think you might fail. But here's the thing, Shawn. If you'd really, genuinely loved me, you would've been able to tell me about your misgivings. We would have been able to work through them together. Because when you truly love someone, you won't let anything get in the way."

"I never lied to you, Jamie—"

"No, maybe you never did. Maybe you believed everything you said—all the dreams we planned to share together, everything. And maybe you even believed that you loved me. But that doesn't change one fact. Deep down, Shawn, you just didn't love me enough. And that's the real reason you didn't show up that day."

She had her explanation now. It was really quite simple, quite devastating. She'd been in love with a man, so in love that she hadn't been able to see any of the warning signs. All this time she'd wanted the truth from Shawn when she should have been able to see the truth herself: he simply hadn't loved her enough. The knowledge left her with a terrible emptiness inside.

Would she ever be able to trust any dream again?

KAITLIN BOUNCED FROM one foot to the other in excitement. Ever since she'd met Ana at the pet show—Ana with the turtle—she'd been just a bit more vibrant. And today there was definitely a motive for excitement. Jamie and Kaitlin were going to surprise Eric again.

"Do you think he's figured it out?" Kaitlin whispered. "Do you think he'll be here on time?"

"Even if he's late, we'll wait for him. We can't get this show on the road without him."

Jamie and Kaitlin were at Saint-Anne's Heron Airfield, going through the preflight checklist. Kaitlin held the clipboard and carefully marked off each item. "Nose gear…check. Landing gear…check."

"Good job, sweetie."

Kaitlin smiled. Just that…she smiled. No reservations, no complications at this particular moment. An expression of simple happiness. Jamie gave an answering smile, but it was a front. The ache inside her threatened to overwhelm.

How would she tell Kaitlin that in only a few days she'd be leaving?

She'd gotten what she came for. She'd traveled all the way to Saint-Anne to find her runaway groom and she had the explanation she'd needed. It was not a comforting explanation, by any means, but it *had* told her the truth. Now she had to get on with the rest of her life, whatever that might be.

She had to leave Eric and Kaitlin Sinclair behind.

"Are you okay, Jamie?"

"I'm fine, honey. Just fine." Now she was the one concealing her true emotions. This little girl had come to mean so much to her, it was time she faced the emptiness of leaving Kaitlin….

Surely Kaitlin would do well without her. Jamie had done what she could. She'd just given Kaitlin a nudge in the right direction. Jamie could be satisfied with that one accomplishment, at least.

Jamie's pep talk to herself wasn't working. She felt distraught. She'd lost her illusions and now she was about to lose Kaitlin. And Eric, as well.

"Are you sure you're okay, Jamie?"

"Just fine, sweetie."

Eric's truck pulled up. He climbed out, came toward Jamie and Kaitlin and gave both of them a suspicious perusal.

"More and more mystery," he said, loosening his tie. "An urgent call from Mrs. B., telling me I have to leave Seattle and come home. My pilot and copilot need me right away."

Kaitlin bounced up and down. "We're kidnapping you, Dad! It's all set. We're going to fly away together—and we're not going to tell you where."

Jamie had to admit that Eric was once again a great sport. He looked at the two of them and finally put up his hands as if in surrender.

"I give," he said. "Looks like I'm being...*dad*napped."

Kaitlin's brown eyes shimmered in delight.

A short time later they were in the air, soaring with the clouds. Jamie had hoped that the sky would work its usual magic on her and that she'd be able to soar above her problems, as well.

No such luck. The emptiness and the longing could not be escaped.

Everyone else on board, however, seemed quite able to

relax. Kaitlin and Isabel fulfilled some of their copiloting duties but then retired to the cabin, where both stretched out for a nap. Planning surprises could tucker you out.

Eric took the second seat beside Jamie, but in a few moments he was dozing off, too. He'd been working overtime on the current big venture for Sinclair and Sons—the Garrett project—and apparently he hadn't been getting much sleep. Jamie herself had been the victim of sleepless nights lately.

After twenty minutes or so, Eric stirred and opened his eyes.

"Have a good rest?" she asked all too politely.

"Actually, yes. Having you as pilot is the best cure for insomnia I know."

"That doesn't sound like a compliment."

"It is," he assured her. "Usually I can't fall asleep on a plane. It's the control issue, I suppose, along with a dose of superstition, the idea that if I'm watching out for trouble, none can happen. Idiotic, I know, but it's kept me weary-eyed and yawning on too many flights. When I'm flying with you, Jamie, it's different. I know you're in charge, in control, and that's enough."

Too bad she didn't feel in control when it came to her emotions. Everything in her life seemed upside down.

"I'm wide-awake now," Eric said, "and I have to admit I'm glad you got me away from the office. I've been asking myself a lot of questions about work lately. Number one—why am I negotiating a loft development where other people get to use their imaginations but I'm essentially crunching numbers."

"You said it, not me." Her gaze strayed toward his

profile. Well-defined features that had been molded, it seemed, by restlessness and discontent.

"It's a worthwhile project," he said, as if trying to convince himself. "Three buildings in all, a combination of living and work space, green construction, energy-efficient, all the bells and whistles."

"For crying out loud," she said. "You've outgrown your work and you know it. You'll be on the verge of admitting it, only to pull back. Honor and family duty win out every time until you start thinking about your dreams again. That's why you haven't even asked where we're going today. Tomorrow, of course, you'll feel guilty you took a break and you'll be right back at the grindstone. Push and pull. It's so admirable and yet so…so aggravating."

He gazed at her with a hint of amusement. "Thanks for setting me straight, Jamie."

She wished she could set herself straight. Outside the sky was the color of pewter, a metallic shade that reminded her of all the murky, unanswered questions in her life. She had Shawn's explanation now, but all her dilemmas regarding Eric continued to plague her.

Eric spoke, as if sensing the direction of her thoughts. "You still haven't told me," he said quietly. "What happened with you and my brother?"

She glanced back to make sure Kaitlin still slept on. "I really can't talk about it, Eric." How could she say the words out loud to him? His brother simply hadn't loved her enough. Maybe there was something in her that made men leave—first her father and now Shawn. "I just can't talk about it," she repeated.

"If he hurt you again—"

"I don't appreciate *how* Shawn went about it, but I'm starting to realize that walking away from me was the right thing for him to do. He knew that our marriage wouldn't work out. How can something like that work when you're not really, truly, completely in love—"

He gazed at her. "Are you talking about yourself or about my brother?"

Her hands tightened on the controls. What could she say now? Of course she'd loved Shawn. She'd been ready to embark on a whole new life with him, take any risk—*her* emotions hadn't been the ones lacking. Unless her own feelings were illusion. If that were true, where did that leave her?

"I just can't talk about it, Eric," she said for the third time. He looked at her intently, as if to draw more from her, but then he subsided. And so they flew onward, only silence between them.

VOICES AND LAUGHTER drifted from a large pavilion situated outside the city/county complex of buildings in Whitfield. Music could be heard, too, evoking the Caribbean with drum and Spanish guitar. Several people milled about the pavilion, children as well as adults. It was a party, and the entire city had been invited to join in on the fun.

"Okay," Eric said, apparently no longer able to contain himself. "What gives, you two?"

He'd continued to be a good sport all through the flight to Whitfield. He'd gone along gamely, hadn't even questioned the cherry-red sports coupe waiting for them when they'd landed. Eric hadn't even objected when they'd driven to the Whitfield house so that Jamie and Kaitlin could change into their "dress-up" clothes.

Now, though, as they walked toward the pavilion, it seemed they'd tried Eric's patience to the max.

"What gives?" he asked again.

Jamie nodded at Kaitlin. "You're on," she said.

Kaitlin took a deep breath and said the words she'd practiced several times. "You need a push in the right direction, Dad. We're here to do some…some…"

"Networking," Jamie whispered to her.

"That's right. Networking."

"We just happened to learn that Whitfield is celebrating Founders' Day," Jamie said. "Founders' Day… hmm, think about it. What better time than this to remind the mayor and every member of the city council that the Whitfield bridge is a historic landmark desperately in need of restoration?"

"A historic landmark," Kaitlin echoed. "In need of restoration."

Eric studied his daughter. He studied Jamie. And the expression on his face…

There was a tenderness for Kaitlin that took Jamie's breath away. As for the sensual way he was looking at her—that didn't even bear thinking about.

Jamie pulled her gaze from Eric's and nodded at Kaitlin. This was the signal. They both stepped toward Eric and gave him a nudge in the right direction.

"Go network," Jamie said.

"Go get 'em, Dad," said Kaitlin.

He knelt down to his daughter's level for a moment.

"Thank you, peanut," he said softly. "Tell Jamie I said thanks, too."

"I'll tell her."

They watched as Eric walked away from them, moving toward the pavilion.

"Do you think he liked our surprise, Jamie?"

She wasn't sure *like* was the right term. They'd really pulled a fast one on him this time. She and Kaitlin had had great fun together this past day or so, planning all the details, once again roping Mrs. B. into the scheme.

"We're getting good at surprises, aren't we, Jamie?"

"Very good. Now, let's go enjoy some of this party ourselves."

"Dad said I looked pretty in my dress." Kaitlin smoothed a pleat.

"Very pretty," Jamie agreed. "You have very good fashion sense, honey."

"So do you." Kaitlin slipped her hand into Jamie's. How easily and naturally she did that now. Jamie wished that neither one of them ever had to let go.

But she would be saying goodbye to Kaitlin so soon. Goodbye to Eric, as well.

"Do you have the sniffles, Jamie?"

"I'm fine, sweetie." How many times could she say that—often enough to convince herself? "Come on," she told Kaitlin, forcing a lighthearted tone. "I see they're serving punch and chocolate cake today. We don't want to miss out."

And so they walked on together, Jamie and the little girl who had stolen her heart.

Chapter Fourteen

Not only did Founders' Day include punch and chocolate cake but also a master storyteller who entertained the children at one corner of the pavilion. Jamie and Kaitlin listened as he told stories of the city's early history—the Native Americans whose name meant "people of the sun," the workers who'd once toiled at the lumber mills, the men who had laid mile after mile of track to bring in the railroad. Kaitlin was enthralled, but at last she could no longer resist the draw beyond the pavilion—an antique carousel brought in especially for the occasion.

Jamie and Kaitlin went to admire the carved horses, and Jamie lifted Kaitlin onto a steed with a streaming yellow mane and curled hooves. The workmanship was intricate, impressive under the chipping paint. The horses had been decorated in old-fashioned candy colors—taffy and butterscotch, licorice and peppermint. Jamie stood back and watched Kaitlin go round and round.

"She looks happy," Eric said.

Jamie started. She hadn't seen him come up beside

her. It had been an hour or so since they'd sent him off with the instruction to "network."

"That's what carousels are for," she said. "Happiness."

"Sometimes, Jamie, you try to minimize your own role with Kaitlin. As if you're afraid to make it seem too significant. Why?"

Because she would be leaving….

Jamie clenched her fingers against her palms. She had to tell him sooner or later—of course she had to tell him. Yet still she delayed.

"Any success, Eric? Any city council members who lent an ear?"

"I went off to schmooze the bigwigs, just as you and Kaitlin told me to," he said. "Had a good talk with the mayor, anyway. She and I are old acquaintances—I knew her when she had braces. Hard to believe she has a child of her own now—and *he* has braces."

"Point taken," Jamie said. "Kaitlin and I didn't really need to go to all this trouble. You could have just picked up the phone and dialed Mayor Julie. Except, I don't think you would have picked up the phone."

"Point taken," he responded. "I'm glad you went to all the trouble. Very glad. I'm looking forward to what you and Kaitlin have planned next—looking forward to the expression on her face when she tries to keep another secret."

Jamie could no longer avoid reality. She simply couldn't.

"I'm leaving, Eric. I'll be in Washington only another few days, at most. I'll leave as soon as…as soon as I can break the news to Kaitlin. As soon as I can clear up a few details. Loose ends."

"Leaving," he echoed.

"It can't be news to you. After all, I've spoken to Shawn. He's told me what I needed to hear, and that was the whole reason for me being here."

His eyes were storm-blue, a color she was not likely ever to forget. "As for loose ends," he said. "Was today one of them?"

She gazed toward the carousel. "Kaitlin's been so excited about your bridge—she's adopted it as her own project. So when Mrs. B. told me about Founders' Day, I knew I had to make one last visit here with Kaitlin...with you."

"So," he said. "Mission accomplished."

"Exactly. That's what you've been telling me all along, isn't it? You kept saying your plan would work—and you were right. Your brother showed up. And your daughter...well, all right, I won't minimize my role with her. I helped her. And now she'll go on."

"End game," Eric remarked.

It was the way things had to be. So why did she hate the idea so much? The idea of never seeing Eric Sinclair again.

Never. She didn't like the word. She didn't like it at all.

Music surrounded her and Eric—music from the carousel as well as from the Caribbean guitar. Other couples were dancing in the grass and along the verge of the pavilion. Eric took Jamie into his arms and held her close in a slow rhythm.

"Don't," she whispered against his shoulder.

"What's waiting for you in New Mexico, Jamie? Not your job, not even a place to live. You can stay here. Why not?"

To stay…in his arms. To stay and dream about a man and a little girl who did not belong to her.

"There's no future for me here," she said tightly. He couldn't seem to find an argument with that, but he drew her a little closer, his hand warm through her clothing. She hated knowing that she'd chosen this dress, a swirl of peach silk, precisely with him in mind. Earlier today, when she'd come down the stairs of the Whitfield house, she'd wanted to see the look in his eyes, a look just for her. She hadn't been disappointed.

She was playing with fire, playing with it even now as she and Eric turned to the music. And, just beyond, the carousel turned, little Kaitlin blurring in Jamie's vision.

With a great effort of will, Jamie pulled away from Eric.

"There's no future for me here," she repeated, staring at him, almost daring him to prove her wrong. He gazed back, unsmiling, intent. But it seemed he had nothing to offer her—no statement to prove her wrong.

She was leaving.

IT WAS, ON THE SURFACE, an ordinary morning, one day after the return from Whitfield. Jamie and Kaitlin took the nine-o'clock ferry into Seattle with Eric. Kaitlin was going to learn how to work the new copier, a most important job. And Jamie…well, that was where the ordinary part ended. She'd made an appointment to see her ex-fiancé at the office so she could return his ring to him. It was one of those loose ends that had to be tied up. She'd been stashing the ring in a drawer, but it was an important detail that couldn't be avoided any longer.

In the reception area of Sinclair and Sons, Eric murmured to Jamie, "Sure you don't want any backup in there?"

That was just what she didn't need: her *fake* fiancé helping her with her *former* fiancé.

"I can handle it. See you guys later." She watched as the dark-haired father and daughter went off together, hand in hand. Kaitlin was doing a lot more of that lately—holding out her hand to others. She would be fine, Jamie thought, smiling at Kaitlin's progress. Everyone would be fine—including Jamie herself. She just had to keep telling herself that, even when she couldn't seem to believe it.

Jamie walked down the hall to Shawn's office. He was immersed in a file-cabinet drawer.

"Stacy, where's that latest spec from Jackson—" He broke off when he looked up and saw it wasn't Stacy. His expression seemed to brighten.

"Hi," he said. "When my secretary told me you were coming, I was very surprised...very pleasantly surprised. You and I—we're not finished yet, are we?"

Typical Shawn, asking her a question that could be interpreted in a variety of ways. Not finished as friends? Not finished as lovers?

There was a pause between them. You tended to run out of conversation when it came to an ex-fiancé. She took the small jewelry box from her pocket, placed it on the desk and turned to go.

"Jamie…wait. We still need to talk." He went to close the door, then came back to face her.

"Shawn, there's nothing more to say."

He gazed at her earnestly. "That's where you're wrong. I've been doing a lot of thinking since…well, since our little discussion. And I'm thinking…we try it again, Jamie. There was something special between us—you know there was. We had something great together, even though I was keeping you at a distance. That's what I'm offering you now…no more distance between us."

She stared at him, shocked at his offer. "Shawn, it's too late."

"No, it's not," he said. "Not at all. Because you were wrong about one thing, Jamie. You said I didn't love you enough. But I do—I love you with all my heart. I guess it took losing you for me to realize that. Jamie… can you forgive me? Can you take me back? And, most of all…will you keep my ring and agree to marry me again?"

JAMIE WAS FINDING IT very difficult to tie up loose ends. Right now she was at the Saint-Anne house, trying to pack up her belongings, but her clothes no longer fit in her luggage. The shopping spree she'd had when she'd arrived had thrown everything out of kilter. In a minute, she'd have to go down and see if she could borrow a suitcase from Mrs. B.

She smoothed her hand over a swirl of peach silk. It

didn't seem fair that a piece of fabric could already be threaded with memories. She seemed to remember every detail of the one time she'd worn this dress—only two days ago, in Whitfield. Eric had gazed at her as if he'd simply wanted to go on looking forever....

But she'd seen other expressions on his face. She could define each of them: reluctant, stern, severe. They belonged to a man who would not easily trust again.

Who was she to blame him? She'd given up on trust herself. Wasn't that why she'd turned down Shawn's proposal yesterday? No matter that he'd refused to take no for an answer.

She sank down into the nearby armchair, momentarily unable to continue. Right after hearing that startling proposal of Shawn's, she'd looked deeply into his eyes and had seen what appeared to be utter sincerity. He'd said that he loved her—and he'd appeared to mean it. But how could she trust him ever again, let alone her own judgment? Especially since she'd spent so much time lately thinking about her ex-fiancé's brother.

She crumpled the peach silk, only to smooth it out again. Now she had not only a fake fiancé but a former fiancé who wanted to change his status to current. Where did that leave her?

More confused than ever. And that was why she had to leave this place. She'd already delayed long enough. She had to leave, had to get some balance back into her life. Tomorrow was absolutely the last day she'd be spending on Saint-Anne.

Last day, last time...those phrases seemed to echo

inside Jamie's mind. The last time she'd given Kaitlin a swimming lesson. The last time she'd told her a bedtime story. A few books remained piled on Jamie's night table. A story about toads and another one about a poor girl and a lonely dragon. There'd been an occasion or two when Kaitlin couldn't sleep and Jamie had allowed the child to snuggle here in the armchair with her. They would read together and then Jamie would lead the sleepy little girl back to her own room. She'd tuck her in, kiss her forehead and say good-night. Almost like a real mom....

Jamie felt that recurring ache inside her. She could not risk staying here and allow her feelings for Eric and his daughter to grow. She feared that her affections where the Sinclairs were concerned would always be distorted by her own need for home and family. Most of all, she didn't trust Eric's emotions. He'd brought her to Saint-Anne to help his daughter, but did he feel anything deep and lasting for Jamie herself? She swept up the books and carried them down the hall to Kaitlin's room. Everything had to go back to its proper place. Everything.

Skirting the basket where Isabel was taking one of her naps, she set the books on a shelf, turned to go and saw Kaitlin hovering at the door.

She couldn't avoid breaking the news to Kaitlin any longer. Jamie had agonized about the best way to handle the situation and had finally decided to wait until today. She wanted to give Kaitlin time to adjust—but not too much time to brood. Of course, who knew if Jamie was making the right decision about anything? Eric had warned her that with children, you never knew how they'd react to difficult news. You just tried your best.

What if her best wasn't good enough?

Jamie sat down on Kaitlin's bed and beckoned the little girl to sit close to her.

"Honey," Jamie began, "how would you like to visit New Mexico sometime?"

"Great," Kaitlin said promptly. "We can fly there. You and me and Dad and Isabel."

"Well, yes, we could do that. But I was thinking of something a bit different." This was even more difficult than Jamie had imagined it would be. "I was thinking, Kaitlin...you could come to visit me in New Mexico."

The little girl stared at her, refusing to comprehend. "But you'll be *here.*"

"No, I won't," she said as gently as possible. "I'm going back to Albuquerque, honey. It's where I live—where I belong. But I'll write lots of letters to you, I promise. We'll talk on the phone all the time and, of course, you'll come to visit me."

Tears brimmed in those large brown eyes, and then Kaitlin burrowed fiercely against Jamie. "Why?" she mumbled.

Jamie gathered Kaitlin close and rocked her in her arms. "Hush, sweetie. Hush."

"Don't leave me, Jamie. Please don't leave," Kaitlin sobbed. Suddenly she wasn't the only one in tears. Jamie found herself weeping for too many reasons: sorrow at leaving, remorse for hurting Kaitlin this way when all she'd wanted was to help. And she cried because soon she'd never see Eric or Kaitlin again. That realization was almost too much to bear.

ERIC AND SHAWN SAT across from each other in Eric's Seattle office. These days, Eric had been neglecting the Saint-Anne one and he felt remiss. Jamie and Kaitlin's refurbishing of it had been a gift to him, and he should be honoring it by using it, enjoying it. What had been holding him back? Family duty, family obligation? Jamie had told him in no uncertain terms that he could no longer let obligation dominate his life. Jamie always did have a way of stating her opinion clearly.

Shawn jiggled his foot, hunching his shoulders in concentration. Eric was reminded of the time when at seven, his brother had rescued a disabled sparrow on the island, commandeering a shoe box from one of the shop owners downtown, then walking all the way home with the bird. Something about the very smallness, the ordinariness of the creature had inspired Shawn; he'd vowed that he would personally nurse it back to health. Quickly, though, the task had overwhelmed him. He'd avoided his new charge, pretending that some other loftier work required his attention. Mrs. B. had been left to call the island's resident "bird lady," a woman who took care of wounded birds. Shawn had been mightily relieved, although he'd refused to admit it. Eric had been relieved, too. At nine, he hadn't been any better at long-term projects than his kid brother.

These days, things had changed and Eric was too good at seeing long-term, Shawn not good enough. You'd think one or the other of them could have learned a little balance.

"In too deep?" Eric asked his brother. Shawn gave him a distracted glance but didn't answer.

"I hear you threw your hat into the ring again," Eric went on. "I hear you popped the question to Jamie all over again."

Shawn remained silent, but his air of remote concentration intensified. Eric, meanwhile, surveyed the financials spread out on his desk. The Garrett project was proceeding, through no enthusiasm of his own.

"Maybe," he said, "you're already regretting that *re*-proposal. You ran out on her once. You know that nobody deserves to be hurt the way you hurt Jamie. The last thing you want to do is hurt her again."

Shawn finally seemed impelled to speak. "I never make the same mistake twice. At least you have to admit that much about me. If she'll have me, I'll do everything I can to make up for what I did. I'll do everything I can to make her happy."

"Thought she turned you down," Eric pointed out.

"I'm not giving up."

"You might not have much time left to change her mind," Eric said. "Yesterday she moved to a room at the Sand Castle." Jamie seemed to see the island hotel as a way station between his house and the ferry. Apparently things hadn't gone well when she'd told Kaitlin about leaving. So now it seemed she was trying to leave by bits and pieces.

So far Kaitlin had not been consoled by these halfway measures.

Eric could no longer abide the financial reports in front of him. "Come on," he told his brother.

"Where are we going?" Shawn always had wanted to know his destination beforehand. During the few family road trips they'd taken as kids, he'd been a pill. He'd invented at least fifty variations on the classic "Are we there yet?" whine.

"Come on," Eric repeated. He didn't wait to see if his brother would follow, just went out into the hallway and punched the Up elevator button.

Shawn made it into the elevator just before the doors closed. They rode to the health club on the penthouse floor. Eric went into the equipment room, where he shrugged off his jacket, rolled up his sleeves, tossed some boxing gloves at his brother and began lacing on a pair of his own.

"Haven't done this is a long while," Shawn said.

"Now's the time."

"You want to beat me up, that it?"

He wanted some exercise. He wanted to do anything that would obliterate the memory of Jamie in his arms. He didn't know how to define his feelings for her. She loved—perhaps still loved—his brother. Eric's rule stood: any woman connected to Shawn was off limits. But it was more than that. After the failure of his marriage, Eric honestly didn't know how much left he had to give. Jamie needed someone who could give her everything.

Could that someone turn out to be Shawn after all?

He and his brother went to the padded area of the room used for stretching exercises. They had the place to themselves. Eric had installed the requisite handball court, the necessary weight-lifting paraphernalia, but there was something elemental about boxing that had always appealed to him, so he kept the gloves and some heavy bags around for good measure.

"Come on, Shawn. Take your best shot."

Shawn feinted left and then swung right, taking Eric by surprise. He ducked just in time. Shawn always had been a good opponent. They'd started boxing in their teens and over the years had vented a lot of aggression with these gloves.

"I want her back," Shawn said, bouncing nimbly on his toes.

"You don't deserve her." Quick jab to the right, avoided by Shawn's deft weave.

"You don't deserve her, either," Shawn said.

Eric couldn't deny that much. Unless he could commit wholeheartedly to Jamie, he should stay away from her. But how did you give your whole heart when you no longer believed in love? If having a daughter as wonderful as Kaitlin couldn't keep two people together, what would do the trick? He and Leah had managed to destroy each other's illusions. The last thing Eric wanted was to fall *out* of love with another woman, with all the inevitable hurt, pain and recriminations. Jamie was entitled to more than that. If he couldn't promise her forever, he shouldn't promise anything at all.

Another feint. His brother was getting too predictable. Eric's next jab made contact. Shawn jumped backward.

"I'll explain to her again," Shawn said earnestly. "I'll make her see."

"Explain it to me," Eric said, "because I sure as hell don't get it."

Gloves up, they were both circling, considering their next strategies.

"I fell for her," Shawn said soberly. "That's it. I fell for her. I knew she was the one, and it scared me. You find the right person and there's nothing left after that. Maybe it'll be great, maybe it won't be. But there's nowhere else to go. You face her, you face yourself, and maybe you won't like what you find."

Eric made contact again and Shawn went down. The instant it happened, Eric knew this wasn't what he wanted. He didn't want to fight his brother, after all. He took off his gloves and kneeled beside Shawn.

"Okay?" he asked.

Shawn moved his jaw. "Not broken," he said. "How about a drink?"

Once Shawn's gloves were off, they went across to the lunchroom.

"I love her," Shawn said. "That's the bottom line."

Eric sipped some more of his sports drink. "Won't change anything, though. She deserves better."

"You keep telling me that. But I really do love her."

More than ever, Eric didn't trust those words. They were too simple, too easy to say. Yet, was his brother sincere?

Eric finished his drink and headed toward the elevator.

"Thanks," his brother called after him.

"For what?"

"For not standing in my way. For not going after Jamie yourself. I knew the engagement was fake all along. You were just trying to set me up."

Eric didn't answer. He went down to his office, where

the financial reports were scattered on his desk, still waiting for him.

It seemed that one way or another he was going to lose Jamie. The knowledge of it reminded him of the last time he'd been boxing with his brother, and Shawn had actually managed to land the big punch. He'd gone down cold.

Maybe he'd gone down cold this time, too.

On one level, he was angry at his brother. What right did Shawn have to hope for a second chance with Jamie? Hadn't he done enough damage—didn't he realize that the only honorable thing to do was walk away? On another level, however, Eric had to admit a reluctant admiration for Shawn. It took courage to go after what you wanted, especially when you'd made a mess of things the first time around.

Eric himself was trying to be honorable, letting Jamie go because he couldn't give her everything and because he didn't believe in half measures. But maybe he wasn't being completely honest. Maybe he wasn't just afraid of hurting Jamie.

Maybe, deep down, *he* was afraid of being hurt again.

Chapter Fifteen

Late that evening Eric heard Kaitlin crying in her sleep, sobbing as if her world had collapsed around her. He went to her, smoothed the hair from her face, the tears from her cheeks. He would do anything for her, anything at all, and yet he could not seem to help her with this.

Once she was sleeping quietly, her little face pale against the pillows, Eric sat beside her for long moments more, searching for solutions. He'd talked to the psychologist often about these nighttime episodes. She said she'd been trying to help his daughter, and yet Kaitlin still battled her private nightmares. He needed an answer. He needed…Jamie.

Eric believed in logic. His daughter had rarely cried in her sleep while Jamie had been here. In fact, Kaitlin had spent several peaceful nights in a row…until Jamie had left the house. Coincidence? He didn't think so.

Finally he switched off the bedside lamp and went across the hall to his own room. Sitting down, he tried to focus once more on the work he'd brought home with him, but it was pointless. He thought about his daughter and wondered yet again if he'd failed her. He was the one who'd arranged Jamie's presence in the house, because he had seen no other choice. His daughter needed Jamie, end of discussion.

Except that it wasn't that simple. In the back of his mind, he'd pictured a possible scenario: Jamie getting back together with his brother, becoming Aunt Jamie and therefore always being part of Kaitlin's life. For a brief second or two he'd been okay with the idea.

Not anymore.

Forget the fact that Shawn had proposed to Jamie all over again. Definitely forget that.

Eric swore under his breath. He stood and paced the room. The one scenario he'd refused to consider was Jamie leaving and his daughter being disconsolate. He was supposed to be an expert at taking the long view, but this time he'd avoided it. He'd known only that his daughter needed Jamie *now.* And now would have to be good enough.

Again, it wasn't that simple. His own questions about Jamie kept intruding. Why couldn't he stop thinking about her? Why couldn't he stop wanting her?

He became aware of soft, almost furtive noises from his daughter's room and went across the hall to stand in her doorway. Kaitlin was wide-awake, out of bed and rooting through one of her bureau drawers.

"Hey, peanut. Can I help you?"

"No, thanks." She made a determined effort to ignore him as she went about her business. She found a sweater in her bureau, brought it over to the bed, folded it carefully and then stuffed it into her backpack. A return to the bureau, this time for a shirt and a pair of jeans. A careful folding job once more—and into the backpack.

"Going somewhere?" he asked conversationally.

"Never mind, Dad."

He came into the room. "If you *are* going somewhere," he remarked, "you might want to think about your slicker. It's rainy out."

Kaitlin looked him over as if wondering just how far she could go with this. But then she took her slicker from its hook and laid it beside her backpack.

He glanced at the kitten curled up on the bed, purring in a determined manner. "I don't know how Isabel will feel about a trip just now. I imagine she doesn't like the rain."

"She'll be okay."

A tough customer, his daughter.

"How about we pack some food for you?" he asked, still in that conversational tone. "I don't want you to get hungry."

"No, thanks."

"You know, sweet pea, wherever it is you're going, I'll miss you. It'll be very lonely without you here."

She ducked her head. "I'm going to see Jamie," she said in a soft voice.

He nodded gravely. "Does she know you're coming? Because we could call and tell her."

"That's okay." Kaitlin examined her bookshelves as if searching for a favorite book to take along.

Eric went to her and knelt down beside her. "How about this, peanut," he said gently. "I'll drive you over to see Jamie. We'll go to visit her, the two of us. Does that sound like a plan?"

She studied him again. And then, at last, she nodded, her mouth trembling as she tried very hard not to cry.

"Hey, you know how much I love you, don't you? I love you with all my heart."

THE KNOCK AT JAMIE'S hotel room door came at well past eleven o'clock. Of course, she hadn't been asleep. She wondered if she could even remember the last time she'd slept peacefully. Pulling on her robe, she padded to the door and looked out through the peephole. She saw Eric Sinclair, dripping rain.

Jamie swung the door open. "Eric, is everything all right—" She glanced downward then and saw Kaitlin, also dripping wet. She drew the little girl inside. Kaitlin was wearing her jungle-animal pajamas, her favorite blue flannel robe, black rubber boots and her yellow slicker. "Oh, honey…"

"Hello, Jamie," Kaitlin said formally.

Jamie slid off the little girl's slicker and shook it out before glancing at Eric, who'd come inside and closed the door. He was carrying a pizza box, which he opened for her inspection.

"Well," she said, "this *is* a pleasant surprise. How on earth did you know that I was hungry for pizza? And not just any kind. Pizza with mushrooms and bell pepper *and* olives."

"We just knew," said Kaitlin.

"Imagine that. How lucky am I?" Of course, there was a story behind this midnight visit, but first things first. She headed to the bathroom and returned with towels for both her visitors. While helping Kaitlin dry off, she tried not to notice how good he looked in his jeans and pullover, his hair curling damply. Tried not to tell herself how much she'd been missing him, missing Kaitlin. Tried not to notice how this plain, no-frills hotel room suddenly seemed to be filled with warmth and color and life.

"You know what would be fun?" Jamie said. "Finding an old movie on the television and eating our pizza while we watch. What do you say, Kaitlin?"

The little girl nodded. And then, so softly she almost couldn't be heard, she said, "I missed you, Jamie. That's why we came."

"I'm very glad you did, honey." Jamie busied herself with getting them all settled so she wouldn't grab Kaitlin and hold her forever.

The room had an alcove with a sofa and television; they switched channels until they found a 1950s science-fiction movie. At first Kaitlin didn't really seem to care what was on the television as she snuggled between Eric and Jamie and ate two pieces of pizza.

Sometime later, when they'd all had their fill, Jamie carried the pizza box to the kitchenette. Eric followed her. By now, Kaitlin did seem genuinely fascinated by the movie.

"Is she all right?" she whispered.

"She is now."

Jamie ran water in the small sink. "I know this is difficult—"

"She needs you, Jamie. Maybe more than ever now. You want to know why we're really here tonight? She was packing up to leave, running away to find you."

Kaitlin tried to run away? Jamie shut off the water. "What on earth are we going to do?"

He shook his head, and once again she saw the pain in his eyes.

"It's my fault," he said. "I'm the one who came up with the whole idea. I'm the one who arranged everything so she could be close to you."

"Because you wanted to help your daughter."

"Trouble is, she still needs help. Your help. It's as simple as that."

"I can't think right now." She shook her head. "It doesn't seem simple at all. It seems incredibly complicated."

"Maybe not." He gazed at Jamie thoughtfully, and she felt a strange sense of foreboding.

"What do you mean?"

"I'm just considering possibilities."

"*What* possibilities?"

"It might be a little too early to discuss them," he said enigmatically, glancing at Kaitlin. "But still we have choices."

She didn't see any good ones.

JAMIE HAD HER suspicions where Mrs. B. was concerned. The next day, Mrs. Braddock called her at the hotel and issued one of her invitations. Not tea this time, just a casual supper, a chance for some "girl talk." Eric knew all about it, but he wouldn't be there, as he and Kaitlin were going to the movies.

Jamie paced her hotel room, debating with herself. To go or not to go... She'd never been indecisive before.

Her confusing emotions, however, had derailed her. She lingered on the island, telling herself it was so Kaitlin could gradually get used to the idea of her leaving.

Who was she kidding? Her own heart wouldn't let her leave. She cared for Kaitlin. As for Kaitlin's dad...well, that was a whole other story. She kept trying to figure out exactly how she felt and only ended in a worse quandary.

Jamie paced some more. It was difficult to think when you hadn't had much sleep. Last night's visit from the Sinclairs hadn't helped her peace of mind; it had only churned up more emotions, more confusion. Seeing Eric Sinclair at her door, helping his daughter "run away" and find Jamie, had almost made her smile despite the gravity of the situation.

How on earth did you resist something like that?

So it was that Jamie parked her rental car in front of the Sinclair house at exactly seven o'clock, walked up to the door and rang the bell.

It was Eric who answered. "Hi."

"What are you doing here?" she asked.

"I live here."

Jamie gazed into his eyes and all her turbulent emotions threatened to engulf her. She felt as if a tidal wave were sweeping her farther and farther out to sea.

"Mrs. B. invited me for a little one-on-one. *You're* not supposed to be here."

"That's funny—because she's the one who's not here. She's on an overnight visit to her sister's. My daughter's on an overnight, too. Ana and the turtle invited Kaitlin and the kitten for a sleepover. After

Kaitlin promised that she would never, *ever* try to run away again, I let her go."

Jamie turned to go. "I know a setup when I see one. Tell Mrs. B. nice try."

"I hate setups, too," Eric said, "but it would be a shame to let all that food go to waste. You should see the spread she left."

Jamie turned back slowly. "Eric, I don't think it's such a good idea, you and me.... I just don't."

"I've done a lot of thinking since last night, too," he said. "We really need to talk, Jamie."

The sense of foreboding had only grown. "About those...possibilities you mentioned?"

"Something to that effect."

She hesitated for a long moment. Undeniably they *did* need to talk. About Kaitlin. About his brother. About... They just needed to talk.

At last she stepped inside the house. Against her will, she studied Eric. He was still dressed from work: jacket, tie, pants the color of slate. With his dark hair curling over the collar of the tweed jacket and that suggestion of the exotic in his strong features, she might easily imagine him as lord of the manor, ready to entertain for the evening. Except that he had only one guest—her.

Jamie had to admit that she'd taken special care with her own attire, choosing her gold-colored sheath and her heeled sandals.

"All right," she said. "Let's talk. Let's figure out what on earth we're going to do."

Eric ushered her into the dining room as she spoke. Food was the last thing on Jamie's mind. She didn't feel hungry in the least, not with her stomach churning, not with every muscle tensed. But Eric did have a point. Mrs. Braddock's efforts should not go to waste.

Come to think of it, Mrs. B. had made quite a few preparations for this evening. Jamie surveyed the table with its two place settings close together. A low arrangement of daisies and yellow roses would not impede conversation. Two candles awaited only a flick of a match, the lights turned down low.

"Unbelievable," Jamie said as the two of them sat down.

"Mrs. B. is indulging in some manipulation of her own," Eric said drily. "She doesn't want you to leave, either."

"What do you want, Eric?" She regretted the question as soon as it was out. She'd never meant to ask it—and ought to have known she wouldn't get an answer. He merely sat there with a dissatisfied expression. Then he rubbed his neck—she wasn't the only one suffering from tense muscles.

"You've been doing that a lot lately," she commented.

He gave her a glance no doubt meant to discourage her from questioning him further.

"For goodness' sake," she said, "you really need to relax. Just take off your jacket and leave the rest to me." When he'd complied about the jacket, she positioned herself behind his chair and matter-of-factly began to massage his shoulders.

"You're good," he said after a moment.

She'd fully intended to keep the situation impersonal. Unfortunately it wasn't working out that way. Her hands on Eric, the heat of his skin radiating to her even through the cloth of his shirt... She could just imagine touching him like this every night, being with him.

Jamie backed away hastily. "Anyway, you get the idea. Start relaxing."

It was a relief when they retreated to the kitchen. Eric heated Mrs. Braddock's summer-squash soup and pulled the salad from the fridge. Other details took Jamie's attention, such as the crusty homemade bread that needed to be sliced, the vegetable-and-tofu casserole that she had to take from the oven when the timer sounded.

Jamie found it soothing to focus on culinary matters. She poured the bubbling soup into bowls and served generous portions of the casserole on plates. Eric gave the tofu a wary examination and disappeared down to the wine cellar. He emerged a few moments later with a bottle of Burgundy.

"Not sure what goes with tofu," he said. "We'll have to experiment."

They carried food and wine into the dining room and sat down together. Almost like a real couple....

Eric filled her glass. "What's bothering you, Jamie? Is it being here with me when you're still wondering about giving Shawn a second chance?"

She disliked his attempts to analyze her, yet found herself answering his question.

"I think he may actually love me," she said, her voice taut. "At first I wondered. I thought...well, I thought he was just being competitive with you. After all, you said the two of you were competitive, didn't you? But maybe..."

"Maybe he loves you." Eric almost seemed to be speaking to himself.

When it came down to brass tacks, though, how could she be certain of anything ever again? How could she trust her own emotions when they ran riot within her any time she was near a Sinclair man?

Jamie tried to eat. The squash soup was delicious, lightly flavored with herbs. Too bad she couldn't enjoy it more.

"It's possible," Eric said, "Shawn's the one for you. Maybe you should…accept him."

Her stomach was clenching all over again. "Is *that* one of the possibilities you wanted to discuss?"

"Think about it, Jamie. You loved my brother once. It sounds as though you still do. You owe it to yourself to find out."

"Unbelievable," Jamie muttered again. "Mrs. B. is playing matchmaker for you and me. Now *you're* playing matchmaker for me and Shawn."

"You came all the way here to find him," Eric pointed out. "Turns out you didn't just find him—you got him back. Now you have to decide…do you *want* him back?"

Jamie set down her spoon. This whole situation was maddening. "I don't know anything anymore. But I have a suspicion what *you're* doing. You're trying to tie up your own loose ends. You figure that if Shawn and I get back together, that'll solve everybody's problem, won't it?"

"Aunt Jamie," he said discontentedly. "Hell."

Jamie pushed back her chair. "Don't you see what you're doing?" she demanded. "You're searching for a logical solution to this whole sorry mess. Logic isn't going to cut it, though. Your brother has asked me to marry him—again. Meanwhile, you're still not over your divorce—not by a long shot—yet you and I are supposedly engaged. We're attracted to each other in spite of all our best efforts, and neither one of us has a clue what to do about it. Can you straighten out any of that? I sure as hell can't!" She scrambled to her feet, grabbing bowls and plates.

"I'll take those," Eric said.

"I can do it," she told him grimly.

They both ended up transporting the dishes into the kitchen, wasting most of Mrs. B.'s fine dinner. Jamie filled one of the sinks with sudsy water and furiously began washing a plate.

"If you want to throw the dishes, go ahead," Eric told her. "Might be therapeutic."

She turned off the faucet with a yank and swiveled toward him. "I don't want to feel this way. As if everything—everything's in turmoil—"

"I don't want it, either," he said. Then he took her into his arms and kissed her.

She tried to resist at first, tried to deny her longings, but it was impossible. With a sigh, she surrendered herself, her fingers twining through his hair, her mouth opening to his. Their bodies seemed to meld together, finding a fit that was wholly natural. Until this moment, she had denied herself. She had refused to admit that this was her most secret, most dangerous fantasy of all.

There was no denying it now.

She made one halfhearted attempt to argue with her own desires. She lost the argument. When she and Eric broke apart, both of them breathing unevenly, she didn't say a word. She simply gazed into his eyes, saw how the blue of his had darkened to smoky gray. He seemed to be asking an unspoken question of his own.

"Yes," she whispered.

He took her hand and pulled her from the kitchen. Silently they went into the dining room, stopping to extinguish the candle flames. As dusk gathered around them, they went up the stairs, down the hall and into Eric's bedroom.

She had never been in this room before. She'd passed the door countless times, but she'd made a conscious decision not to peer inside. It had seemed a measure of self-protection. Now, as he switched on the bedside lamp, she asked herself one more time if she was doing the right thing. Her heart beating wildly, she glanced around, looking for anything that might help her find reason. A scattering of books here and there; a plaid robe hanging from a hook; an exercise bike in the corner; an old, well-worn Persian carpet beneath her feet. A functional place, no excess, no pretension of any kind. Certainly not a place to lose her common sense....

Eric came to stand before her, waiting, allowing her to make the next move. *To hell with common sense.* She went into his arms again. They strained together as if there could never be enough of this moment.

His hands moved over her back, but she was the one who reached behind and tugged at her zipper. Eric helped her and the dress fell away from her shoulders. Another clasp undone and a final barrier of lace had been vanquished. She heard the intake of his breath as he gazed at her.

"Beautiful," he said, his voice husky as he drew her closer yet.

Chapter Sixteen

Buttons. At the moment, their one purpose seemed to be unbuttoning.

Jamie took her time. If she was known for her impatient nature, tonight she would take her time. And so she treated each button of Eric's shirt with the care it deserved. She felt the quick rise and fall of his chest under her fingers.

"You're driving me crazy," he murmured. He framed her face with both hands, kissing her. She explored his chest as the shirt came undone. The muscles, the dark hair curling there, the breadth of his shoulders as, at last, the shirt fell to the floor.

They sank down on the bed together. A belt was unbuckled, more scraps of cloth were discarded, sandals were unstrapped and shoelaces were untied. So much undoing…Jamie's undoing. Eric's fingers caressed her, tantalized her, dared her to be bold. She couldn't stop now, not with this ache of need and desire so deep inside. Eric's legs tangled with hers. She arched against him, refusing to disguise her desire. Honesty was in her nature, too.

He touched her, finding her most secret places. She

gasped in wonder and, for a moment, she did try to hold back. Surely she could not be this indulgent.

"Let go," he murmured against her cheek. "I'm with you." With those words, the sensation cascaded all through her, leaving her warm and pliant and trembling.

"Eric," she whispered. "Please."

Their bodies joined, and now he was the one to be enticed, taken to that exquisite moment of surrender. There was unexpected delight for Jamie, too, a feeling so intense she cried out.

Afterward they lay together content, the light from the single lamp falling over them.

"So beautiful," Eric murmured as his fingers traced a path down her throat. "If you knew…how long I've wanted…"

"How long *I've* wanted. But wanting's dangerous," she said, wishing she could keep reality away from this moment just a little longer.

"It can lead to this." His mouth on hers gently.

"What are we going to do, Eric?"

"More of this." He drew her against him, kissing her again. Her body responded instantly, and when the alarm bells sounded inside her head, she silenced them. She rested in Eric's arms and surrendered all thought of the consequences.

THE FIRST STREAKS OF dawn lightened the windows when Jamie awoke. She must have dozed, but sleep now eluded her, and rather than wake Eric, she slipped from the bed. Eric's bed.

Her skin flamed as she remembered the night they had

spent. *Repeat performance* did not even begin to describe it. She had never been so…wanton. So indulgent.

She retreated to the window seat, taking Eric's robe and drawing it about her. Leaning back, she watched the sky lighten and tried to divine her own emotions.

"Come back to bed."

She gave a start that was almost guilty. "I didn't know you were awake."

"Only now." He'd lifted himself on one elbow, the sheet falling away from that all-too-male chest. His hair was rumpled, his eyes offering promises. If she returned to that bed, she'd truly be lost.

"Maybe," she said, "we should have breakfast."

"Fair enough. I'm hungry—understandably so."

Her cheeks burned once more, especially when Eric stood and every masculine aspect of him was magnificently revealed. He seemed completely unselfconscious as he padded across the carpet. Tilting her chin, he kissed her.

"Can I have my robe?" he murmured.

"That's just an excuse to see me naked."

"Yes."

As if mesmerized, she allowed him to slip the robe down over her shoulders. Another kiss. And another….

She stood rather unsteadily, which was a mistake. He untied the robe and it fell to the floor.

"Not again," she whispered. "We couldn't possibly."

He smiled. "I could, very possibly. But you're right, breakfast first. We need some strength." He picked up the robe and put it on, all the while his gaze lingered upon her. "Don't go anywhere. I'll be right back."

When he'd left the room, she started scrambling for something to wear. She felt too exposed in every sense—physically, emotionally. She found some pajamas draped across a chair back. In a few seconds she'd buttoned herself into the top and slid on the bottoms. She had to roll up the cuffs on both. The silken material, unfortunately, carried Eric's scent—again, utterly masculine, soap and cologne, brisk as a Northwestern forest.

He returned then, carrying a tray of bowls, spoons, soy milk and a box of whole-grain cereal.

"There's nothing normal in the house anymore," he grumbled. "Not even eggs for the omelet I was planning. And who's ever heard of soy milk? What's wrong with cows?"

Jamie couldn't help smiling. She sat cross-legged on the bed, the tray in front of her as she poured two servings of cereal. "We'll survive," she said.

"If you keep wearing my pajamas, that'll make up for a lot of things."

She wished her face would stop burning, but when he looked at her like that…

"Let's eat," she said, her voice wavering unexpectedly. She poured the soy milk and focused gratefully on the cereal. It was hearty, to say the least. Eric leaned in to kiss a drop of milk from her lips. The feel of his mouth on hers made her forget all her doubts and worries.

Maybe that was why Jamie didn't hear the bedroom door open until it was too late. She pulled away from Eric…and saw Kaitlin in the doorway.

"WHAT ARE WE GOING to do?"

Jamie didn't know why she kept asking that question since Eric was no help at all. He didn't seem to have any answers, either.

They'd conducted as much damage control as possible. It turned out that Ana's mom had dropped Kaitlin home earlier than expected due to an extreme case of homesickness. And since Kaitlin had her own key, she'd used it. Not surprisingly, since Kaitlin had been looking for her dad, the first place she'd looked was his bedroom.

After some scrambling, Jamie had quickly steered the subject to Kaitlin's sleepover adventures—the board games she and Ana played, the movie they'd watched until well past bedtime, the ice cream snack Ana's mom had allowed. It appeared that her night had been a fair success.

Unfortunately Jamie and Eric had indulged in their own version of the sleepover.

Jamie's skin heated all over again just thinking about it. She was like someone with a fever that couldn't be cured.

"What are we going to do?" she repeated, even though she knew it was useless.

She and Eric had convened in the den downstairs, after Jamie had hastily exchanged the pajamas for her gold-colored dress and sandals. Eric wore jeans and a T-shirt. For the moment, Kaitlin was safely ensconced in the kitchen with Mrs. Braddock.

"It's all too humiliating," Jamie muttered. "The evidence we left behind...dishes half-washed, the wine bottle on the table... Why didn't we just rent a billboard and announce to the world that we were going to bed?"

There. She'd said it out loud. She'd gone to bed with Eric Sinclair. She didn't have any excuses, though. She couldn't even blame the wine. She'd had only a glass and a half, not nearly enough to cloud her judgment. Her good sense, nonetheless, *had* deserted her.

Eric propped his elbows on the arms of his chair and gazed at her. She suspected instantly what he was imagining.

"Eric…don't."

"It was a good night, Jamie," he said, his voice low and husky. "A very good night. I think we can both agree on that."

"Of course it was a good night. It was a fantastic night. It was…it was—"

"Fantastic," Eric agreed.

If he kept looking at her like that, she didn't know what would happen. She'd probably go into his arms and try for fantastic all over again. She was that susceptible to him. "We may have caused irreparable damage to your daughter."

"Aren't you being a little melodramatic, Jamie?"

Even the way he said her name sent a wayward shiver of awareness down her spine. He spoke differently to her now, a subtle sense of possession in his tone. And why not? He knew her in the most intimate of ways….

"Dammit." She pressed her hands to her cheeks, but she couldn't cool them. "I'm not overdramatizing in the least. Given the circumstances, what we did was wrong. And then to be caught like that—"

"Think about it," he said reasonably. "In a normal, ordinary household, children might often see their parents in a similar situation. A wife wearing her husband's pajamas. Both of them eating healthy cereal."

"Don't joke about it."

"I'm not joking. I'm merely pointing out the facts. As far as Kaitlin's concerned, she didn't see anything unusual. If anything, she was reassured. What she saw was Jamie, back home, where Jamie belongs. I'm willing to bet nothing else really registered with her. That's the way it should be. Parents going about their usual prosaic business, providing a foundation of security that kids hardly notice. Yet it's crucial, that foundation—"

"Stop," Jamie said. "Just stop." She took a deep breath, trying in vain to control her agitation. "You keep talking about husbands and wives and parents. But I'm not Kaitlin's mother. And I'm certainly not your wife. This *isn't* a normal, ordinary household."

"I don't suppose it is." Eric leaned back in his chair and considered her reflectively. "Maybe," he said, "we should turn it into a normal, ordinary household."

"Eric...what are you saying?"

"It's simple, Jamie. I'm asking you to marry me—for real, this time."

All she could do was stare at him and listen to the pounding of her own heart. "You're serious...."

"Completely," he said, his voice utterly calm. "I've given this considerable thought. Think about it, Jamie. You and I...we have feelings for each other. Perhaps we're not able to break them down logically just yet, but they exist nonetheless."

Jamie couldn't sit any longer. She jumped up and went to glare out the window. She clenched her hands.

"Good sex—fantastic sex—that's still not a basis for marriage, not by far."

His eyes had turned that smoky blue-gray. "It's a damn good beginning. And so are the other feelings between us. Okay, I'll admit they're not clear yet, but that doesn't mean we can't figure them out—we'll have a long engagement. Marriages have been based on far worse—such as falling in love with someone you don't really know at all."

She frowned at him, annoyed at his reference to her debacle with Shawn. An engagement that had left her alone at the altar.

Eric went on. "We have another reason to get married, Jamie, a very good one. Perhaps the best of all. Kaitlin."

If she started to think about that little girl, she would truly be lost. Her judgment would be clouded completely.

Truth was, she'd already fallen in love with Kaitlin. But had she also fallen in love with Kaitlin's dad?

NEXT AFTERNOON, JAMIE sat in the grass at the Whitfield park, gazing at the old bridge. There was something soothing about its graceful arches and weathered stones. The bridge had endured so many years, seeming to suggest that Jamie could endure, as well.

She wished she had more confidence in her ability to carry through difficult situations. In reality, she now had *two* supposedly genuine proposals of marriage on the table, something she never thought possible.

Of course, she'd already said no to Shawn—whether he was listening was another matter. But she had not given her answer to Eric. She'd hoped to retreat to the island hotel for a few days so that she could have solitude and time to think; unfortunately, however, she was still company pilot at Sinclair and Sons, and earlier today Eric had requested a flight to Whitfield. This time they had traveled without Kaitlin, and he'd been mysterious about the purpose of the trip. He'd simply asked her to fly him here and meet him later by the bridge. They'd agreed on five o'clock—it was now four fifty-nine.

Precisely three minutes later she saw Eric walking toward her, his stride long and confident. He looked like somebody who could conquer the world.

When he reached her, she stood. "Hello, Eric."

"Hello, Jamie." There was a new intensity to him, a new look of purpose in his eyes. She couldn't help wondering what he'd been up to today, but she'd been doing her own thinking and she had something to tell him. It simply couldn't wait.

"Eric," she said. "I've been considering your proposal and I'm afraid that I'll have to say no. Any way I look at it, you're doing this for all the wrong reasons. You asked me to marry you because of your daughter. Perhaps also because you're dissatisfied with your work, and any change seems good right now. Although I hate the thought of it, the competitiveness with your brother probably comes into play, as well—"

"Don't forget the other night," he said. "That's a primary motivator."

She felt her skin warm. "We both have too many unanswered questions," she went on with determination. "That's the point I'm trying to make."

"You're wrong about one thing, at least. I *have* resolved a rather important question in my life. I'm finally doing it, Jamie. I'm taking your advice and following my dreams. I've just been through a slew of meetings and, of course, there are still more obstacles in the way—but I'm going after it. I'm putting in my proposal to restore the bridge." He seemed to savor the words—and he repeated them as if to relish them all over again. "The bridge, Jamie." He swept her into his arms and kissed her exuberantly.

Eric Sinclair exuberant? She rested both hands on his chest. For a second or two she allowed herself to indulge in him. His warmth and strength, his assurance and undeniable virility.

"That's wonderful. It's absolutely wonderful!" She repeated, caught up in his enthusiasm. After that, she just couldn't resist. She kissed him without reserve, just to show him how much his news meant to her, too.

A delicious moment later they broke apart. The light in Eric's eyes remained. He gestured as he spoke to her, telling her all his plans. She listened to the tone of his words, the intensity and happiness behind them: "Load balance restored…prestressed concrete to bolster the existing system…and, of course, the cast-iron lanterns completely rehabilitated…"

It seemed utterly natural when, much later, they wandered from the park and into the grove of ponderosa pines. Here the evening shadows deepened around them as they walked hand in hand. They came to the gate in the brick wall, passed through and crossed the lawn to the two-story house with mullioned windows.

Inside, they opened the small cooler that Mrs. B. had packed for them. She'd provided her usual excellent feast—smoked salmon this time, chilled on ice. Endive salad. Pears and ripe plums for dessert. Eric and Jamie sat together outside on the porch steps, relishing each bite. It seemed entirely natural to be here, holding hands companionably. For the first time in a very long while Jamie felt herself relaxing, accepting the possibility of happiness that she glimpsed. When a silence stretched out between her and Eric, that seemed comfortable, too.

She gave a languorous sigh. "I think I love you, Eric." When those words came, unbidden and unexpected, they seemed as natural as everything else passing between them. Perhaps this was her answer at last, the confusion banished. "Yes, I do believe I love you," she said.

She was so caught up in the wonder of it that she didn't notice how Eric's hand had stilled upon hers.

"Was it so terrible, what I said?" She was dismayed to hear her voice shaking. "Loving you—is that getting just too damn close?"

He raked his fingers through his hair. "Getting close is what we've been doing all along, Jamie."

She wasn't so sure about that. Suddenly, though, she *was* sure of one thing—her feelings for Eric were different than any she'd known before. Different, certainly, than what she'd felt for Shawn. With him, she'd projected her own dreams and hopes. When he'd appeared in New Mexico, he'd molded himself agreeably to her life, her surroundings, but had never revealed himself to her. In the end, she'd never truly known him.

With Eric, it was completely the opposite. She'd landed in *his* life. She'd seen every day how he interacted with his daughter. Nothing feigned there. Just a father trying his very best to do a good job. Questioning himself, worrying and caring and providing. Getting up the next morning to try it all again, with all his heart. Under those circumstances, she'd really came to know the man. And at last she knew what she felt for him.

A real love, a genuine love.

If Eric couldn't say the words to her in return, did that matter so much?

Yes. It mattered a great deal.

"Jamie, we have a connection. You know we do. One that can't be denied."

He had that right.

The question was, did he love her in return? She knew Eric desired her. That he wanted to make a home with her, a home where Kaitlin would always feel warmth and safety and happiness. But...did he *love* her?

Admittedly, she was glad that Eric did not express any emotion lightly. He seemed to analyze his feelings as objectively as possible. You could trust whatever he told you. Jamie herself had come to disparage too-hasty pronouncements of devotion. She'd had that with Shawn, and look where she'd ended up—she'd been a bride without a groom. With Eric, it would unquestionably be different. If he said he would stand there at the altar with her, he would.

But would he ever love her the way she needed to be loved?

After everything she'd been through, Jamie had learned you could reach out with both hands and grab your chance at love—but only if the man you loved did the very same thing. If he didn't, you only had one choice left.

"I'm sorry, Eric," she said, holding back her tears.

Then she did the hardest thing of all. In spite of the dismayed look on Eric's face, Jamie stood and walked away.

STEADY AND SURE, THE airplane hummed its way through bright sunshine. Strangely enough, Jamie had almost forgotten about this dazzling New Mexico sky. Over the centuries, artists and poets had tried to capture the beauty of it, the play of light upon the turquoise-blue. But Jamie constantly found herself thinking about another sky, in the Northwest, where pearl-gray shadows could so quickly obscure the sun.

You're dwelling on it again. You can't help yourself and you know it.

She would not be a defeatist. It had been less than a week since she'd returned from Saint-Anne, and it would take a very long time to erase certain memories. Perhaps they never could be erased.

"This is so cool! It is just so great! Wow!"

The sixteen-year-old girl beside Jamie had a habit of speaking in exclamations. This was her second lesson, and it was getting a bit wearing. Nonetheless, Jamie didn't like to dampen anybody's enthusiasm when it came to flying.

She'd gotten her old job back as a flight instructor in Albuquerque. Her boss was a gentleman of sixty who had four daughters and who'd had the kindness to refrain from asking Jamie too many questions. Jamie could be grateful for that much.

"Incredible! I love this! I really do!"

Jamie could only imagine what lesson number three would bring. She wanted to give some advice: *Don't feel so much so quickly. You'll burn yourself out or get burned, and neither possibility is a good one.*

I should know.

Throughout her lonely childhood Jamie had nurtured that illusion of a real family, a real home. When Shawn had come along, he'd seemed to match the illusion so easily and effortlessly. Then she'd met Eric Sinclair, a man who allowed no illusions. The way he made her feel…

Confused. Off center. Aching inside.

The confusion had started the moment she'd bumped her head on that windowsill and he'd taken hold of her. He'd treated her all along as an inconvenient nuisance, yet he'd also kissed her and made love to her….

She had to stop thinking about him. Surely leaving Saint-Anne had been the only solution. She and Eric had already caused enough harm. No further evidence was needed than one of Jamie's more painful memories: the tear-streaked face of a little girl who didn't understand *goodbye.*

She needed you and you let her down.

Jamie tried to silence the regrets. Leaving Saint-Anne *had* been the right thing to do. Someday Kaitlin would understand.

Someday can be a very long time.

"This is so amazing! I can't wait until tomorrow when I can fly again!"

For Jamie, tomorrow only seemed to hold more bewilderment and uncertainty.

Would she ever see clear skies again?

Chapter Seventeen

The piece of paper in front of Jamie was crinkled from a heavy application of watercolor paint. It showed a dark picture, a small figure with teardrop eyes and a wavering line where a smile should have been. A little girl adrift.

"That's me…without you," said Kaitlin on the other end of the phone line.

Jamie closed her eyes as she listened to Kaitlin's soft, mournful voice. She'd receive the picture in today's mail, courtesy of Mrs. Braddock, and she'd immediately called Kaitlin. It hadn't taken much coaxing for Kaitlin to talk about her painting…and about how much she missed Jamie.

Children were known for overstating their emotions. That was practically the definition of being a kid—indulging happiness or pain until a new emotion swept the old one away.

This is different and you know it.

Jamie tried to reassure Kaitlin. She asked questions about the swimming pool, about Isabel, about her best friend Ana.

Then Jamie got to the heart of the matter.

"Honey, I think we'd better have a talk." For some time, she'd been thinking about what she wanted to say to Kaitlin. She just hadn't been able to find the right words before, but now was the time.

"What I'm about to tell you…well, it's about me. About when I was a girl not much older than you. About *my* divorce. My dad left, and I thought for the longest time he would come back. When I finally realized that he wasn't, I thought my heart would break."

Kaitlin didn't say a thing in response, and Jamie could only stumble along, searching for the best way to comfort her.

"Sweetie, my dad never quite knew how to make things right. Eventually we did start to see each other again, but we couldn't seem to repair all the damage between us. I'd go visit him in Colorado whenever possible, but it was never really enough. The point is, I lost my father in too many ways. I can't let the same thing happen to you.

"Honey, your mom loves you more than you will ever know. Maybe she doesn't know quite how to tell you that all the time…and maybe you don't know quite how to tell *her* what you're feeling, but she's your mom, Kaitlin. And so I want you to promise me one thing. Go see your mother. Just go see her."

Jamie stopped, almost out of breath. She didn't know if she'd reached Kaitlin—perhaps she couldn't understand any of this yet. How *did* you understand when you were so young and so worried that maybe your mom didn't love you anymore? So worried that you wouldn't even risk going to see her?

"I will, Jamie. I love you," the little girl said at last before handing the phone quickly, it seemed, to her dad. Another pause; no doubt he was waiting until Kaitlin had left the room.

"Hello, Jamie."

"Hello, Eric." She gripped the phone. They hadn't spoken since she'd left. She had no idea what to say to him.

"Kaitlin wants to know if she can call you tomorrow."

"Of course."

"Jamie... Seems to me that after all we've been through together, you should realize—more than anybody—that I deserve and *require* an explanation."

"Don't do this to me, Eric. You know why I left."

"Do I?"

She missed Eric. She missed his daughter. But without those three all-important words from him, she could never go back.

"Do you love me, Eric?"

"You know that I care for you, Jamie. And maybe things would be different now between us if I could say the right words. Give you reassurances, promises. But words don't make a relationship. I learned that during my *first* marriage. I said all the rights words back then. Meant them, too. But they stood for something unrealistic, something impossible."

"It's clear to me now," Jamie said. "It seems you don't believe in love anymore, Eric."

When Eric seemed to have no answer for her, Jamie forced herself to go on.

"How *is* Kaitlin doing?"

Another pause. "Not well," he admitted. "She

seems…sad. She needs you. There's something about you, Jamie, that reaches her and gives her courage."

She didn't know what to say after that. Any way she looked at it, the situation was impossible.

"I have to go, Eric."

"Busy night?"

Actually, it wasn't busy at all. She'd probably spend it sitting in one of those lumpy armchairs in Mom's living room, reading a book or a magazine.

"I have to get up early tomorrow. Lots of activity at work."

"New students?"

"Learning to fly is quite the thing these days. People seem to think it will open up a whole new life for them."

"A new life," he said. "Everyone wants that at some point."

"It never really is new, though, is it? We carry the same baggage from one situation to the next."

Again, he had no argument to offer. After that, there really wasn't anything to do but say goodbye.

"I knew you'd get your heart broken all over again."

Jamie glanced up to see her mom standing at her bedroom door.

"Not now, Mom."

"I warned you not to go. I only wish that you had listened to me." Mom's voice floated across the room. Caroline Williams was a pretty woman, the silvery streaks in her red hair quite becoming, but she was barred from looking soft by her absolutely clear-eyed approach to the world.

Jamie still didn't have an apartment in Albuquerque

after letting her old one go while making plans for her wedding to Shawn. Until she found a place, she'd have to stay with her mother. Predictably she and her mother were already beginning to grate on each other's nerves.

"Only one good thing has come out of it all. You've learned. You won't let it happen again."

Jamie moved restlessly to the window, where she could see the first rose and violet of sunset. She couldn't seem to sit still anymore. Even flying no longer soothed her. In the past, soaring into the sky had always given her perspective, had always helped her rise above her problems—literally and figuratively.

Not anymore.

"You wait and see. Eventually the pain will go away. You'll have wisdom, and that's more important than anything else."

Wisdom...hardly something that would warm you on a cold night.

"I worry about you, Jamie. I love you."

For just a second Jamie wondered if she'd heard correctly. Never, in all her memory, had her mother said those words to her. Hearing them now meant more than anything to Jamie. Her mother prided herself on not being demonstrative, yet as Caroline stood there, her expression filled with concern, Jamie realized how much her mother truly did care for her.

"I love you," Caroline said again, as if testing the phrase and finding it more and more to her liking.

It seemed that everyone knew how to say the words and mean them. Everyone except Eric Sinclair.

"I love you, too, Mom."

ERIC CRUMPLED A PIECE of paper and tossed it across his office, missing the trash can by a few inches. Shawn picked up the ball and tossed it in with a swish.

"You really blew it this time, didn't you?" asked Shawn.

Eric shrugged.

"No point in pretending," Shawn pushed. "You're afraid that you've lost Jamie for good and it's killing you inside."

His brother had a way of rubbing salt into the wound.

Shawn leaned against Eric's desk, gazing reflectively out the window. "Do you ever wonder, Eric, why you and I keep messing up with women? I've been thinking about it a lot. Could be our less-than-idyllic family history. A dad nobody could ever please, a mother who went into retreat our entire childhood. Sometimes when we were kids, I'd cause trouble just to see how far you'd go to clean up the mess."

"Thanks," Eric said.

"Maybe," said Shawn, "I was just trying to get attention—yours. I couldn't get Mom's attention and I sure didn't want Dad's."

Sometimes it had felt as if it was just the two of them, trying to make sense of their cockeyed family. They'd only been children, they hadn't known how to make things work, but in their own way they'd looked out for each other.

"You really love her, don't you?" Shawn asked.

Eric's feelings for Jamie had been deepening every day, but until this instant he hadn't known how to put them into words. He realized that he'd been falling in love with Jamie since the moment he'd met her. He'd resisted his emotions, then rationalized them and finally offered Jamie a proposal of marriage that didn't offer nearly enough. He'd still been afraid of the ultimate risk—giving his heart.

It was too late for fear now. He loved her.

With effort, he returned to the matter at hand. "This will be a new chapter in the legacy of Sinclair and Sons. Your chapter, Shawn. You can make of it anything you choose. You have my full support. You don't need to follow Dad's direction...or mine. I know you don't like the grand scale of what this business has become. I'm starting to doubt myself whether my vision was even the right way to go. But now it's up to you. I'm stepping back."

"I haven't even given you my answer yet," Shawn said.

"There is no answer to give. The business will be yours to run however you like. I'm stepping back. Sell it if you like. These days, I don't care so much about the family legacy. I care more about...the family."

As he spoke those words he wondered what he was doing still sitting here. Wasn't it time he created the family he really wanted?

A short time later Eric waited in the truck outside Leah's house. Actually, it had been *their* house, but he'd never particularly cared for it. He found the pseudo-Greek columns to be a bit much. Leah was the one who'd wanted this place because it reminded her of her childhood home. Eric had believed that was a strike against it right there. Nonetheless, clinging to the past had seemed very important to her, and Eric had finally agreed to the house.

He was considering past history himself. His conversation with Shawn had put him in mind of that. For example, he wondered how many times over the years he and Leah had failed to make decisions that were truly a collaboration. They'd too often gone their separate paths. How did you find balance in a relationship between dependence and independence?

The door opened, and Kaitlin and Leah came down the walk toward him. All the old uneasiness was there between them. You could see it in the stiff way Leah held herself and the equally restrained manner of his daughter. Did children always imitate their parents in all the wrong ways? At least now, though, Kaitlin was reestablishing a relationship with her mother.

Eric got out of the truck. Kaitlin gave him her usual solemn glance and climbed into the passenger side.

"I need to talk to you," said Leah. She moved a short distance away from the truck so Kaitlin wouldn't hear. Eric followed.

"I'm worried about her," said Leah.

"So am I."

"She's just not responding to anything I do. You may not realize this, Eric, but I really do want to be a good mother."

He knew she wanted that. She was sincere. And yet…somehow she made it come down to reassurance. She wanted him to tell her that she *was* a good mother, that it wasn't her fault.

What would Jamie do? She wouldn't want to be placated. She was too impatient for that, too confident. She'd simply see the problem at hand and try to solve it.

Lately all of his thoughts had been going back to Jamie.

"Are you listening, Eric?"

"Yes, I'm listening." He was looking, too, seeing all the years he and Leah had spent together, all the misunderstandings and missteps. Maybe if he got married again, he'd make those same missteps.

Then again, maybe not.

Jamie wasn't Leah. It was that simple. He'd cataloged the differences before, but he'd never felt the truth of it deep inside, the way he was feeling it now. Jamie was different, and whatever he had with her would be different, too.

Sometimes the answers were so blindingly simple you couldn't see them even when they were in front of you. Yes, he would make mistakes with Jamie, but that was the beauty of it. Perfection not required.

The past with Leah truly was over.

"Why are you smiling so much?" Leah asked suspiciously. "What did I do that's so funny?"

"Nothing. But I have to go." He turned away from her and then turned back again. "I wish you only the best, Leah. Whatever you do next with your life… only the best."

"That almost sounds like goodbye," she called after him.

He climbed into the truck and pressed his foot to the accelerator. Kaitlin remained silent beside him. Eric realized what he had to do now. He pulled over after only a few blocks so he could give his daughter his undivided attention. For once, he needed to let Kaitlin know exactly what he was feeling. Maybe that had been the problem in the past—he had never let her know.

"Kaitlin," he began, "you and I need to talk."

Her eyes widened a fraction, but she continued to regard him warily.

He struggled to find the right words, to find his way. "There are a lot of things I've never told you before. I haven't really told you just how much you mean to me. You're my little girl, and that's everything."

She gazed back at him intently. Was he getting through to her? Impossible to tell. Besides, he just didn't have enough practice at this type of thing.

That would have to change—starting now.

"I love you, Kaitlin," he said. "Maybe I've messed up as a dad, but I love you."

Still those solemn brown eyes observed him without a hint of reaction. He was messing this up, despite all good intentions.

What would Jamie do?

Somehow considering that question gave him inspiration. "Kaitlin," he began again, "I love you as much as all the elephants in the world."

Her eyes widened a fraction more.

"I love you," he said, "as much as all the whales and dolphins and starfish in the ocean."

Her mouth twitched.

"As much as…" He hoped he wasn't running out of inspiration.

"As much as all the butterflies and birds and bumblebees?" she asked.

"That much and more," he agreed. The burden he had been carrying for so long suddenly seemed just a bit lighter. "Here's the deal, Kaitlin," he went on. "It's about Jamie. Seems I've made a mess of things with her, too.

Maybe she doesn't even want to talk to me anymore. But I want her back—and I know you do, too. Maybe it's already too late, but we have to try."

His daughter stared at him for a long moment. He reached over, put his arm around her and gave her a big hug.

"I love you so much, kiddo. What do you say you and I put our heads together and try to get Jamie back? We show her that we need her as much as—"

"As much as all the monkeys in the trees," Kaitlin said with a smile. "Go for it, Pops."

JAMIE NEEDED A MOMENT of respite. It had been one week since she'd left Saint-Anne. "I'm going out for some fresh air, Mom."

"Don't be long. The green beans are almost ready."

Her mother tended to overboil everything; she'd served spongy green beans throughout Jamie's childhood. Jamie escaped out the door and walked down the street, past houses in Southwestern colors of terra-cotta, cinnamon and sand. In New Mexico, if you couldn't afford a house of adobe brick, you duplicated the look with a stucco facade. Jamie had always found that charming before, but now her mind was filled with images of other exteriors. The shingled walls of an island home. Or two-story redbrick with mullioned windows, in a city where a decaying stone bridge needed restoring.

Did every thought have to return to Eric Sinclair? She'd done the right thing in leaving. It would save her a lot of turmoil later…even if she was in turmoil now.

She was starting to sound like Mom.

Jamie quickened her pace. She waved to elderly Mrs. Silva, out puttering in her cactus garden. Mrs. Silva waved back.

"Feeling better, dear?"

Jamie wondered if all the neighbors knew about her bumpy romantic history. Probably. They constituted her mother's support system. Perhaps Caroline Williams refused to allow a man into her life, but she did have friends on this street, people who would watch out for her.

It still wasn't enough to warm you on a cold night.

Jamie wondered if she would become exactly like her mother. She'd have her work, she'd have neighbors and friends, but she'd be alone when it was time to turn off the lights. After her foray among the Sinclairs, perhaps that would be all for the best. There were worse things than being alone.

Jamie walked even faster than before. Keep moving, that was the idea. Get the blood coursing, the heart pounding. Except that she didn't need exercise for that. Her heart pounded whenever she thought about Eric, which was pretty much all the time.

"Damn!"

"What was that, Jamie?" called Mr. Hayes from his front porch. He was another longtime resident of the neighborhood and he was always on the lookout for burglars—despite there not being a burglary on this street in twenty years. Jamie waved to him and kept moving.

She'd turned down another street, headed toward the park, when a car pulled up alongside her. It stopped and a man climbed out. Eric.

For one crazy moment Jamie wondered if she'd

conjured him up from her deepest imaginings. She was tempted to walk up to him and poke him to see if he was real.

Eric wore jeans and a T-shirt and he looked wonderful in the setting sun. He also looked disgruntled.

"You're a difficult person to find, Jamie Williams."

All she could do was stare at him. Her heart, oddly enough, was no longer pounding. It beat at a normal, ordinary pace, even though this was scarcely a normal, ordinary moment.

"It took some doing to find you," he told her. "Your mother would only say you were out for a walk."

Mom was cautious that way.

"Are you going to say hello?" he asked.

She didn't know what she was going to do, so she continued walking. Eric fell into step beside her. Unwillingly Jamie took in every facet of Eric's masculinity: the breadth of his shoulders under that favorite T-shirt, the dark hair that waved stubbornly back from his forehead, the smoke-blue eyes that could be arrogant and warm by turns….

With effort, she forced her gaze away from him. "To what do I owe the pleasure of this visit?" she asked.

"I wanted to talk to you."

"Why not just an e-mail or a call?"

"What I need to tell you has to be said in person," he informed her.

They'd reached the park by now, and Jamie sat down on one of the benches. Eric took a seat beside her. A roadrunner balanced itself on the adobe wall nearby. The bird fluffed its feathers, long tail quivering, long beak opening and shutting. Jamie was reminded of a speaker who'd just stepped up to the podium but couldn't decide what to say.

Eric reached up and placed his hand against her cheek. "I love you, Jamie," he said. "I love you as much as…as much as all the stars in the sky. And I can't live without you."

She gazed at him in wonder. It seemed impossible to hope…

"I want to spend my whole life proving how much I love you," he said. "I promise you that I'll make up for lost time. I kept telling myself that I no longer believed in love, but in reality I was afraid of making another mistake. It took me a while to realize that holding back from you was the only *real* mistake. Can you forgive me?"

"Oh, Eric, I was afraid, too."

"No more fears, Jamie, not for either one of us."

"That's a promise to keep," she murmured, so filled with joy that she scarcely knew what to do next. Eric, however, knew exactly how to proceed.

"Will you marry me…again?" he asked huskily just before he took her in his arms and kissed her with all his heart.

"I will," Jamie said. She knew she was definitely getting ahead of herself, but she couldn't wait to start her new life with Eric and Kaitlin.

It seemed she finally had everything she needed. The man she loved—the man who loved *her.* And a little girl. The perfect family at last.

Epilogue

Three years later

The twin-engine turboprop with blue-and-yellow racing stripes was a versatile craft; it served well for Sinclair family journeys. The voyage at hand was a particularly special one: a flight to the small city of Whitfield, in Washington's Inland Empire, for the dedication of a bridge newly restored by Eric Sinclair.

"Have a good nap?" Jamie asked as Eric stirred beside her in the cockpit.

"Never can doze with anyone else at the controls."

They gazed at each other for a long moment. "Happy?" Jamie murmured.

"With you…always."

"Total honesty," she reminded him. "Sometimes it drives you crazy having a two-year-old who's discovered *no.* Not to mention a ten-year-old who's into soccer, birthday parties, slumber parties, pool parties…"

He glanced back to where Kaitlin was entertaining her brother Benjamin. The little boy's shrieks of laughter attested to her success.

"How you ever slept through that," Jamie told him, "I'll never know."

"I get enough sleep deprivation at home. Hazard of parenthood."

They'd shared all the ups and downs—the long nights, the trips to the emergency room, the school plays, the hugs that could melt your heart. Sharing had become the hallmark of her life with Eric. Their lives were filled with every happiness. Eric was no longer a reserved man and he showed her just how much he cared for her everyday.

She smiled at him. "I love you," she murmured, because those three words could never be said enough.

"I love you, too, Jamie Williams Sinclair." The tender look in his eyes held all the promises they'd made to each other. He reached out and clasped her hand in his.

They spent much of their time at the shingled house on Saint-Anne Island, but the two-story brick house in Whitfield had become more and more the family home. Shawn would be meeting them there today, with his latest girlfriend in tow. This one just might be serious...but with Eric's brother, you could never be sure. Shawn was quite busy these days downsizing the family business, Sinclair and Sons, giving it that unique personal touch of his.

Mrs. Braddock would be the only one not present at the festivities this afternoon because she was taking a vacation in Hawaii. Apparently she believed that the Sinclair family was finally on the right track and she could afford to take time for a few adventures of her own.

"The bridge is finished," Jamie said to her husband. "What next?"

"The world."

And that was exactly how it felt as the plane soared through the pearl-gray sky. The whole world waited for them.

* * * * *

Experience entertaining women's fiction about rediscovery and reconnection—warm, compelling stories that are relevant for every woman who has wondered "What's next?" in their lives.
After all, there's the life you planned.
And there's what comes next.

Turn the page for a sneak preview of a new book from Harlequin NEXT.

CONFESSIONS OF A NOT-SO-DEAD LIBIDO
by Peggy Webb

On sale November 2006, wherever books are sold.

My husband could see beauty in a mud puddle. Literally. "Look at that, Louise," he'd say after a heavy spring rain. "Have you ever seen so many amazing colors in mud?"

I'd look and see nothing except brown, but he'd pick up a stick and swirl the mud till the colors of the earth emerged, and all of a sudden I'd see the world through his eyes—extraordinary instead of mundane.

Roy was my mirror to life. Four years ago when he died, it cracked wide open, and I've been living a smashed-up, sleepwalking life ever since.

If he were here on this balmy August night I'd be sailing with him instead of baking cheese straws in preparation for Tuesday-night quilting club with Patsy. I'd be striving for sex appeal in Bermuda shorts and bare-toed sandals instead of opting for comfort in walking shoes and a twill skirt with enough elastic around the waist to make allowances for two helpings of lemon-cream pie.

Not that I mind Patsy. Just the opposite. I love her. She's the only person besides Roy who creates wonder wherever she goes. (She creates mayhem, too, but we won't get into that.) She's my mirror now, as well as my compass.

Of course, I have my daughter, Diana, but I refuse to be the kind of mother who defines herself through her children. Besides, she has her own life now, a husband and a baby on the way.

I slide the last cheese straws into the oven and then go into my office and open e-mail.

From: "Miss Sass" <patsyleslie@hotmail.com>
To: "The Lady" <louisejernigan@yahoo.com>
Sent: Tuesday, August 15, 6:00 PM
Subject: Dangerous Tonight
Hey Lady,
I'm feeling dangerous tonight. Hot to trot, if you know what I mean. Or can you even remember? ☺ Look out, bridge club, here I come. I'm liable to end up dancing on the tables instead of bidding three spades. Whose turn is it to drive, anyhow? Mine or thine?
XOXOX
Patsy
P.S. Lord, how did we end up in a club with no men?

This e-mail is typical "Patsy." She's the only person I know who makes me laugh all the time. I guess that's why I e-mail her about ten times a day. She lives right next door, but e-mail satisfies my urge to be instantly and constantly in touch with her without having to interrupt the flow of my life. Sometimes we even save the good stuff for e-mail.

From: "The Lady" <louisejernigan@yahoo.com>
To: "Miss Sass" <patsyleslie@hotmail.com>
Sent: Tuesday, August 15, 6:10 PM
Subject: Re: Dangerous Tonight
So, what else is new, Miss Sass? You're always dangerous. If you had a weapon, you'd be lethal. ☺
Hugs,
Louise
P.S. What's this about men? I thought you said your libido was dead?

I press Send then wait. Her reply is almost instantaneous.

From: "Miss Sass" <patsyleslie@hotmail.com>
To: "The Lady" <louisejernigan@yahoo.com>
Sent: Tuesday, August 15, 6:12 PM
Subject: Re: Dangerous Tonight
Ha! If I had a *brain* I'd be lethal.
And I said my libido was in hibernation, not DEAD!
Jeez, Louise!!!!!
P

Patsy loves to have the last word, so I shut off my computer.

* * * * *

Want to find out what happens to their friendship when Patsy and Louise both find the perfect man?

Don't miss
CONFESSIONS OF A NOT-SO-DEAD LIBIDO
by Peggy Webb

Coming to Harlequin NEXT
in November 2006.